BOARDROOM M

GRETCHEN KIRKPATRICK

Boardroom M

Copyright © 2020 by Gretchen Kirkpatrick

ISBN: 978-1-7349526-0-5 (ebook) 978-1-7349526-1-2 (paperback)

Printed in the United States of America

www.gretchenkirkpatrick.com

To Ben and Adelaide

I you

BEGINNINGS

TONIGHT WOULD NOT BE A repeat of last night's adventure. Misha Campbell hurried into the restaurant to escape the cold evening that threatened to freeze even as the cherry trees were preparing to bloom. On her athletic five-foot-seven frame, she'd donned a sexy but demure red dress and a thick wool coat that the hostess took from her.

Misha followed the hostess through the bustling D.C. Saturday night dinner scene. Jeff sat in an alcove on a plush settee. Misha went to slide into the booth opposite, but Jeff patted the space next to him, so she sat there instead. As she smoothed her cocktail dress, her hand grazed his thigh. She could feel his heat through the wool pants, prompting a memory of what had transpired less than twenty-four hours before.

Misha appreciated a certain amount of space between herself and others, along with the ability to make eye contact easily. Jeff, however, preferred to close the gap at every chance, putting his company off-kilter with his proximity. With his lovers—and there'd been many—he sat so close that they'd forget everything else. Tonight, Misha would prefer a comfortable distance between them instead of the overwhelming sensation of his six-foot-five body against hers. She looked at his gold-flecked brown eyes, then took in his slim-cut suit. Misha realized she was staring. She looked at the place setting before her, trying to erase the memory of her fingers in his salt-and-pepper hair from the night before.

"I got the package," she said, pulling a brown-paper parcel from her purse.

Jeff opened it slowly, revealing a box of cigars. "We'll have to smoke these later." He tossed the box and wrapping across the table. "How was your day?"

He seemed so casual, as if he sensed Misha's growing discomfort and was languishing in it. They'd been friends for years, intimate friends, but something was different. Misha found herself craving him more than usual. She must be ovulating. But he was acting differently too: somehow overly loving and attentive.

"I thought you said I was picking up a lighter?" Misha then wondered why she'd said this—she didn't particularly care what Jeff had Max put together for him. As long as it wasn't a package of heroin, what did it matter?

"Look at it this way: sometimes, the truth is fluid. On the one hand, it's true that you picked up a package for me that was supposed to be a lighter. I'm now in a position to offer you a job, which wasn't true until the lighter turned out to be a box of cigars. And none of these words provide you with any objective truth at all. So, let me say it this way: tonight, we're going to get very, very drunk, and come morning, we'll switch to Bloody Marys."

"You really do like to hear yourself talk," Misha said, tucking a loose strand of hair behind her ear.

She looked around. Her eyes flickered as a stranger a few tables over slid his hand under the skirt hem of a woman on his left. The woman pretended to laugh at something a man opposite her said as she uncrossed her legs. Maybe this seat would allow Misha some amusement, now that Jeff had decided to be obtuse.

This couple was carrying on a tryst in the middle of a restaurant, and Misha was interested to see how it would play out.

Jeff had more to say, and Misha rejoined at "… working in a mostly ambiguous position where you'll frequently need to make decisions without any support. I can get you a substantial amount over what you made as a professor, but you'll have less control over your hours and will likely work well over sixty hours most weeks. And the work is lonely, even when people surround you. Ready to say 'no' yet?"

"No," came out of her mouth, even though she thought *I don't care* and *please don't make me think tonight—I can't take any more.* "I got an email today."

"I imagine you got more than one."

"Stop being annoying. It was a rejection from Clemson. I'm running out of colleges to be rejected by." Her throat started to tighten, so she chose to say no more.

"That's what I'm saying, Misha. I have a job I can offer you." Jeff smiled at her, but his eyes set in an expression of firmness.

"Georgetown has a position for me?"

"I said the position pays better than what professors make." He spoke as if trying to keep his temper with an unruly teenager.

"I want to be a professor. Can you get me my job back? That's all I've ever wanted to be, and now that's gone."

"Not exactly."

"Then thank you, but I'm not interested. What *does* interest me though is what we can do to distract me from the failure I've become. You're my best friend. Cheer me up." Misha smiled. Her mood had suddenly shifted from sadness to something like joy.

But Jeff ignored her and returned to his subject. "Like I was saying, the lighter was what I requested, but since Max sent the cigars, I have something to offer you."

"Lighters… cigars… truth? Have you been smoking something

you want to talk to me about?" She looked down, catching herself spelling out "lighter' in the condensation from the water glass. Since elementary school, whenever she was listening, she would trace out dialogue in hidden spaces with her fingers.

Jeff laughed. He guaranteed nothing, and there always seemed to be something up his sleeve. So, Misha sat back, pressing her shoulders into his arm stretched along the back of the seat, and gave herself over to whatever the night had to offer.

"We need drinks, garçon!" Jeff waved down the waiter.

Oh my god. What will this mean when it comes to the food? Misha feared that unless Jeff stopped his cocky attitude, their meal would contain additional, unwanted ingredients. But the waiter rushed over, chuckling. Jeff's apparent rudeness was a joke built between the two of them over the years.

"*Oui*, Professor Martin, what can I do for you?" The waiter winked at Jeff.

"Bring us two Four Roses Old Fashioneds, please. And then two more every thirty minutes for the next two hours. Oh, and a bottle of—no, on second thought, just the Old Fashioneds. And bring whatever food you think goes well with that. We'll eat anything. Thanks."

When the waiter left the table, Jeff started talking about his day, why he loved this restaurant, and a hundred other charming nothings. It was as if everything he'd said a moment before had never happened. But like so many times before, Misha just went with it. Things were often far more fun and manageable when she allowed Jeff to control the planning.

Misha let the noise from the crowded restaurant envelop her as background music, while Jeff continued to charm her. She knew that his change of topic and ordering of so much alcohol wasn't an accident. What job could he possibly have in mind that would require her to be drunk before considering it? He was a linguistics professor of distinction at Georgetown, where he did intensive research into machine learning applications. She couldn't imagine how anything connected with that would require her to be fortified with alcohol first.

Misha's eyes returned to the strangers across the room. They were maintaining an excellent impression of good behavior from the waist up, but below the table line, things were starting to pick up significantly. No-one else in the restaurant seemed to notice. Nor did anyone seem to see the woman excuse herself from the table, appear to touch hands with the waiter, and then drop a piece of paper on the table next to where Misha was sitting before entering the ladies' room.

Jeff sighed but said nothing as he watched a man in a navy suit walk by and pick up the paper. He would have to deal with their weak tradecraft, though he smiled as he noted that Misha had watched the entire transaction from beginning to end. She had the qualifications to move forward.

He must put all his focus on Misha because, after all these years, it was difficult to fool her. And if he hoped to keep her alive, then he needed to lie to her a little bit longer. The drinking would help, but he had to stay focused. He wanted to tell her what she was watching, but that couldn't happen yet. He reminded himself that what he was about to do was necessary and needed precision timing. They'd been friends for over ten years, and he'd taken protecting her very seriously. If love was a thing he could feel at all, then that must be what he felt for Misha. So he took another breath and concentrated on this version of his cover.

The next round of drinks arrived. Jeff returned to good spirits, continuing to regale Misha with amusing stories of his life. He noticed that her finger was spelling on the table, noting critical points as he spoke. It was a strange habit but mostly harmless. He found it endearing.

Misha busily traced the words "ten," "University of North Carolina," and "love" on the table, as she and Jeff recounted all the things that friends do. They talked about their first meeting in Chapel Hill and about their colleagues back then. Jeff thought about how he'd known of Misha long before their official meeting. He wished tonight was the night that he could finally tell her why they'd met. But, again, timing and planning were vital for success, so he knew it still wasn't possible.

He imagined their first meeting from her perspective. He'd stopped by during her office hours to discuss a thought experiment on the role of popular culture in the development of the brain. He'd asked her how she would examine the ways in which cooperative and individualist societies show their values through the media and, in turn, how the media's output influences the neural development of the next generation. It was just that level of questioning, somewhere between utterly pretentious and impossible to study, that got Misha's attention. And led to dinner that lasted eight hours. After that, their friendship was secure, and Jeff gained two things: he achieved his mission, and he got a best friend that he'd always dreamed of. Misha, though, believed at the time that she'd found her future husband, which still made them laugh now. Although Jeff loved her as his best friend—and as his job—the idea of settling down with *anyone* gave him hives.

An hour later, Jeff took a deep breath and began again, "I'm about to tell you things you're never to discuss again. Ever! It wouldn't go well for either of us if you did. If you understand, nod twice." Misha did as requested, then looked around—was someone filming a scene for the sequel to *The Firm* or *Snowden*?

Jeff was wondering if she'd drunk enough. He hoped he wasn't showing his concern on his face, around his eyes. "It's funny that you did that," he said, laughing at Misha's glance around the room. "No-one's listening to us."

"So why did you tell me to nod twice?"

"I'm trying to gauge how drunk you are. And watching you freak out amuses me." He played the ass to keep her focused on the message and not on his gaze.

"Drunk?" She looked at the table where the couple had been fooling around, but they were gone, and she hadn't even noticed. *Yep, I'm drunk.*

"Good work. Keep it up." Jeff smiled and winked at Misha as he squeezed her shoulder. "I'm going to talk hypotheticals with you. Think of a human resources department for a company: they keep the organization full of the right mix of people. Sometimes, they need full-time employees, and sometimes they need contractors et cetera. The trick is not to get the best person for one task or field but to find people with skills that work well together. Every once in a while, a unique situation comes up where a recruiter sees an opportunity to take on an innovative approach. *That* is the greatest achievement—to know you've put together a crew of amazingly talented humans who go on to make something impressive and new. Do you follow so far?"

"You sound like a spy or Tony Robbins. Are you my life coach or are we ordering martinis?" She laughed too quickly at her joke and knew she was slipping into drunken oblivion. Tomorrow morning she was going to need more than a Bloody Mary. "Look, Jeff, I so appreciate you. In the last few months, I've lost everything I worked for, and now here I am, wearing cute clothes and hanging out with my best friend. But you can't fix this, though I appreciate the attempt." Misha shrugged her shoulders. "I saw Officer Elliot today." She was done saying no and trying and hoping it would all make sense. Now she was ready to do whatever the fuck life put in front of her—at least that was what the Old Fashioned on the table was saying.

"Elliot found you today?" *That wasn't an ideal outcome,* Jeff thought, feeling the worry starting to build in the micro-expression around his eyes. He looked down at his drink, willing his face back into the mask of a happy drunk. Hopefully, he could handle that officer through back channels tomorrow.

"We played catch up."

"Okay, that… your ability to engage people is a useful talent. But just no. He's such a distraction. And you dicked him over, so I'm guessing he wasn't in the best mood." *That was the thing about Misha: she was impossible to walk away from.* Max saw to it that she'd never grow conceited, but the way he went about this left her unaware of her effect on others. She seemed to see everyone so clearly, except herself. The woman lived in a rare and odd type of bubble.

"You should have seen the way he flipped me off after he threatened me. Positively charming," Misha smirked.

"You're a snarky bitch when you're drunk. God, I've missed you. I'll take care of things with Elliot tomorrow."

The waiter returned with more drinks. They smelled divine, like a library of old books but with the muskiness of sexual promise.

Jeff continued, "Tonight, we have to get drunk, as I need to take you in, and it's the easiest cover. Sorry, love, but it's bottoms up from here on." He was already regretting what he had to do by the end of the night. But Max had told him it was the only way. To protect her, he needed to get her safely into the belly of the beast. After all these years, Jeff didn't see a point in second-guessing Max now, but it didn't stop the knot growing in his stomach at the thought of sending Misha into enemy territory, without warning.

"What do you mean 'get drunk'? I'm already there!" Misha giggled. She had an impossibly low tolerance of alcohol, which Jeff was well aware of. Then she started to think: *something must be off if he needs me to drink more.* But it was too late for thoughts like this—she was already drunk enough that she wouldn't be able to refuse more.

Jeff wasn't kidding about the amount of drinking he wanted them to do. Misha went from drunk to very drunk to *oh-my-god-what-plane-of-consciousness-is-this?* drunk. As usual when drunk, she had moments of extreme clarity, like waking from a long night of dreaming. A moment in an Uber with a driver who wore the cutest fedora. Jeff rambling on some more about the job. Then a blur of blue and green movement that took over and swirled through the night like a cotton candy tornado. The clouds parted temporarily, and Misha found herself in a dive bar next to a woman who'd won an Olympic medal for Russia in the '80s. Misha slurred out a question about steroids. The Russian laughed. Then there was a clown, or they talked about a clown, or maybe the news was showing a Trump tweet. But that part was hazier.

What came back in bits and pieces to Misha over the next few days was her admission to the ER for a banana bag. No Bloody Marys in the morning, just drug-induced hydration. Shortly after the needle, she watched two very tall, very stiff men in scrubs walk towards her bed.

One of the men added something to the IV line. Misha tried to chase out the fog in her brain to see them more clearly. The tall man looked familiar. He made eye contact with her for just a second, but it was long enough for Misha to recognize him—he was the same man who'd waited on them at the restaurant.

The other man kicked up the brakes on the bed and began to wheel her down a hall. She started to feel very tired. Her vision blurred. Something deep inside told her to fight and try to get away. But a much louder voice was thankful for the coming darkness and the escape to oblivion. By the time she was pushed through the next set of doors, she was completely unconscious.

Jeff awoke the next morning agitated. His best friend would be waking up in a new life and, for the first time, had no-one to protect her. He fought off the urge to get drunk and call that sweet guy from the Embassy of Argentina. Then he resisted the urge to go and rescue her from the danger. Instead, he got up and started planning how he'd sort out the Officer Elliot issue and that crap information exchange from the night before. Jeff wouldn't tolerate this level of weak tradecraft in his network.

CHAPTER 1

IT WAS A PERFECT NIGHT for seduction. The cold February air forced people to walk closer, huddling together against the salty ocean breeze pushing between San Francisco's buildings.

Misha had taken her wife to the city for a chance to reconnect. She hoped that if she showed her appreciation, they'd be happier.

Misha started the night by taking Immie to their favorite Italian restaurant off Market Street. A restaurant where the chef pickles the vegetables and makes everything with love… and olive oil. Misha picked this place for Immie as a reminder of their special times in the past. It seemed like the best place to thank her wife for her patience and support over the long months of Misha's fruitless job search. It wasn't easy to stand by someone who'd lost her job and reputation in such a public way, but Immie had done that with so much love and strength. Misha knew she had to remind Immie it was worth her effort. As they shared an appetizer, Misha struggled to find her words.

"Thanks for coming out tonight. I know things haven't been great, but you've really been there for me, and that means a lot," Misha began.

Almost instantly, Immie shifted in her seat. "Let's not talk about that tonight," she said, then reached out her hand and placed it on Misha's. "Let's go get into trouble". Immie's eyes twinkled and her golden hair shone under the lights as she mentally flipped through all the crazy nights they'd had in this town over the years.

"This is important, Immie. You make me feel valued even when I don't." Misha started tearing up. Maybe Immie was right: they were barely off the BART and only on the first course. The deep conversation could wait until after dinner. Misha settled into silence.

"Remember when we snuck into the speakeasy with the help of an Uber driver and a flirty bouncer." Immie needed a night of romance and adventure with her best friend. She couldn't take one more night of discussing feelings or watching Misha spiral into self-doubt.

"Yes, I could've gotten us arrested that night. I can't believe you let me talk you into that."

"How can you remember it like that? We *owned* the city that night." Immie's eyes sparkled as she smiled at Misha. Immie mentally walked down the dark corridors to the stage where she and Misha did the Charleston with actresses in garish make-up and sequined dresses. "We need more nights like that. Let's do it tonight."

"Immie, they're probably sold out tonight. Let's enjoy dinner as the two of us. I want you to know that I love you."

Immie studied Misha for a long moment. She could see that Misha was hidden far away. Misha did this sometimes, create a vision of how something was supposed to go and then refuse to waiver from it. This was happening more often now: Misha forcing everything into the plan she had in her head. It was like she thought she could stop anything bad from happening ever again if she planned enough. Immie found it stifling.

"Right. We can't do *that* tonight." Immie studied her wife to see if she would take the opportunity to come up with a new adventure. But Misha seemed to take the sentence as agreement that their best, most riotous nights were gone forever.

The restaurant suddenly felt chilly to Immie, so she pulled her jacket back on and waved down the waitress to bring them a bottle of pinot noir. Immie decided that she'd fortify herself for another night of loneliness with Misha.

The two women ate in silence. They'd occasionally look up from their plates at each other and the rest of the restaurant. Neither dared to speak. Misha didn't want to upset Immie, and Immie didn't want to start a fight in public. Immie did, however, want to get drunk, so she drank as much of the wine as she could.

By dessert, Misha knew she'd fucked up again. All she wanted to do was show Immie all the love she had for her, but somehow, she'd offended her again. Misha said without looking up, "I thought we could walk down to the pier, but it's cold. And you seem tired. Do you want to go home to bed?"

Immie wanted to scream. Misha wasn't listening or paying attention.

"No. No, Misha I will *not* go to the pier. I'm not tired. I want to go and *do* something. Eating and listening to you tell me I'm amazing because I let you walk around like a ghost of my wife isn't fun. Please let's just *do* something." Immie wasn't exactly yelling, but she was loud and animated, as one can be after half a bottle of wine.

"Tonight is supposed to be about *you*. Not me and my bad ideas."

"I *love* your bad ideas. I live for your spontaneity. I want *you* back." Immie couldn't take this conversation one more second. "You're paying the bill and taking me to Caldera now."

"No. I see you're upset. Let's go home and talk about it."

"Fuck your talking about it. I'm heading out that door now and catching an Uber. Decide if you're coming with me or going home."

Immie stood up, took a swig from the wine bottle, and walked out. Misha froze. This wasn't going well, and Immie was drunk. It might make everything worse if Misha went with her, but she couldn't let Immie wander the streets of San Francisco drunk and alone. Misha threw her credit card down on the table and ran out the door to follow her wife. *I'll have to come back and get the card tomorrow.*

Caldera Bar used to be a favorite of the Beatniks, where people from all economic brackets could rub shoulders. It used to be Misha and Immie's favorite bar too. And ten years before, they'd had their first date there. Imogen Thomas and Misha Campbell discovered a plethora of shared interests over multiple rounds of drinks. The night was the start of a passionate love affair. Since that time, every adventure and misadventure in the city included a stop at Caldera for at least one round. Tonight, Immie wanted Misha to remember those nights and that relationship. However, Misha was feeling more and more afraid that anything she'd say or do would push Immie further away. Both of them knew the significance of the moment, but neither felt equipped to cross the growing divide.

They ordered their drinks and headed upstairs to the loft. Immie went to the bathroom, leaving Misha alone and nursing her default emotion, sadness. She couldn't help but notice how shitty and disgusting the bar was. Through the window, she could see a homeless man's camp. *No-one deserved to live on the streets, on public display. How can we possibly think it's okay for any human to live this way?* Misha's mind darkened and shifted to the comfort of political anger. It was safe to be mad about social issues she didn't cause and was unable to fix. It was more comfortable than the reality that she was blowing it with Immie.

Suddenly exhausted, Misha gazed at the small, round, sticky

table. She picked up her bourbon in an age-frosted lowball glass. As the drink crossed her lips, she shivered, the liquid that resembled rusty tap water lapping at her tongue. She usually only drank rum and Coke here, so this burned its way down her throat.

"Why do I always let her talk me into this place?" Misha complained to no-one. It was a Wednesday, and upstairs was nearly silent at this time of night. She set down her glass and lifted her arm off the table, wondering what could make it so sticky. She shivered again.

Why was Immie taking so long? Misha took out her cell phone. There were multiple notifications on her dating app. Things had been rough since the loss of her job a few months ago, and during one of her long sleepless nights, she'd impulsively set up an account on an edgy dating app. Now she had three chat contacts, all of them into things she found deeply disturbing. These depraved proxy-lovers had been the only ones Misha sustained because of the discomfort they allowed her to feel, instead of the usual horrible emptiness. She'd rationalized that if she enjoyed the chats or started to look forward to them, these feelings would just disappear, like all the things she'd valued or come to expect. Only the darkest and most disgusting tastes made her feel normal. Immie hadn't touched her in over a month, and there was nothing to look forward to, so feeling anything at all had value. Even old joys like showers or hot coffee failed to register as feelings anymore. Life had to be at full volume for that to happen.

The newest message was from a guy who liked to say shockingly violent things, followed by digs at Misha's "husband". His words worked surprisingly well, as none of them were relevant to Misha's actual life. It was a pretend world for a life where Misha could imagine she felt things like fear and excitement. In this sext, he was outlining how he wanted to tie her up in his filthy garage and invite his friends over to do very debased things to her. Misha felt almost nothing as she read it. Still, she replied, faking titillation and spurring him on. The effects were weakening, maybe it was time to dump this conversation and start one with a new stranger.

She then replied to a few other messages. Eventually, there were no new messages to distract her, so she returned the phone to her purse. Immie was still gone. Was she even in the bathroom, or had she sneaked downstairs for another round of questionable drinks? Or perhaps she'd left the bar without Misha noticing?

Would that be the worst thing? We don't have fun anymore. On our first date, I thought this was the most magical place I'd ever set foot in. Immie's shining blonde hair and happy smile pulled me in like all those fake Instagram photos. We sat up here looking out the window onto Columbus Avenue. We discussed everything in the sunny June afternoon. Right then, it seemed that I'd spend the rest of my life listening to that mash-up of Aussie and British English.

Everything about Immie sucked Misha in—her confidence, her laidback grace, and her incomparable beauty. But now it was all heartbreak. There was no connection whatsoever between them. They lived in the same house, but they might as well be in the middle of the Pacific, floating on the wreckage of their love.

Finally, Immie struggled through the bathroom door. She looked more drunk than she'd been fifteen minutes before. She staggered to the table and sat down.

"I'm angry at you," she said, with unfocused eyes.

"I gather. You look mad." *The wine had finally caught up to her.*

"Don't interrupt. I have something important to say."

Misha watched Immie's swaying head and waited. After a few minutes, it was clear that Immie had lost her train of thought and shouldn't have anything else to drink. Misha started to calculate how to get her down the stairs and out the door without starting a fight over ordering another round.

"Misha, you know… I know… I know you don't love me anymore, and I really don't care."

"I *do* love you, Immie." Misha's hand began to trace the word "know" into the greasy table, followed by the word "love."

Immie pouted. "No, you don't. You don't hold me anymore, and nothing is safe."

"I hold you every time you let me touch you." Misha's voice had no intonation. The fight was rote. These were Immie's usual complaints when she was fall-down drunk.

"But you don't *hold* me. You don't mean it anymore. You used to be like the sun, and I could feel your warmth ripple through all of me. But you went away. Where did you go?" Immie began to cry.

Misha hadn't discovered a way yet to extricate herself from this fight, even though Immie's increasingly frequent drunkenness allowed her lots of opportunities to try out different strategies. She could agree with Immie and risk making her cry more, or she could become adamant that she was wrong and risk escalating her anger. In the end, she settled for, "Want to go and sing karaoke?"

"You hate karaoke. You're trying to get me to leave. No. I hate you. Why don't you love me anymore? I never got mad or mean. Why did you leave me? I do like karaoke, though." Immie addressed this with passion to some art on the wall.

Hmm, thought Misha. *That was close to working. "You're* right, and I haven't done enough. I've fucked up in every way possible. I hate karaoke, but I've never hated you. I'm so disappointed in myself. I can't seem to reach you anymore. I hoped tonight I was going to win you back a little. I wanted to show you how much you mean to me. Please let me take you to karaoke. Please let me make a new start. All I can think about is you. I want to make things better." Misha felt a river running unbidden down her face.

Immie's stance softened. Her next "I'm so mad at you" was much more plaintive. She thought about the first time she saw

Misha cry. They'd been dating a couple of months, and Misha's mom had called while Immie was over watching a movie. From what Immie could hear, the two were discussing why Misha had chosen to teach at UC Berkeley instead of a better class of university, such as Harvard. Immie had come to understand the relationship Misha had with her mother—continually trying to please a woman who was impossible to please. Her parents had ridiculously high standards, and until Immie came along, every person Misha dated was an imitation of her parents. It was that tearful phone call that made Immie decide she'd spend the rest of her life with Misha, protecting her from people who didn't understand that she was a total treasure. At this memory, Immie realized that despite her silent vow, she'd become just like all of Misha's other lovers. She felt the numbness of the alcohol as it was wearing off.

"You have every right to be mad at me," Misha said.

"I want you to love me again. I want you to be all mine, but all you do is make everything so depressing. You quit." Now it was Immie's turn to cry.

"I know, but I can fix this. Let me fix it." Misha reached her hand halfway across the table and left it there. Any further might seem like a threat or a demand. *So I wait. I might need to wait for the rest of my life.*

But Misha didn't have to wait too long before a cold palm gently floated like a feather from the air and rested on top of her skin. Her heart screamed and pleaded, *Please don't let go of me. I need you. Please, please stay with me, dearest.* And for the first time in a long while, her desire was met. Immie's hand enveloped hers and squeezed it tight.

Misha wiped the tears with the back of her other hand. "Can I interest you in a few quarters of karaoke?"

Immie cracked a smile at the old joke. "It isn't a sport."

"It is the way you do it, Babe."

Misha had got a tentative truce. She stood and pulled Immie tight against her chest and wiggled her nose into her hair, searching for the faint hint of sunshine and ozone that always clung to it, even in winter. The storm hadn't gone, nor were things better, but this moment allowed Misha to feel something real. Soon the raft would capsize again, and Misha would sink back down to the bottom.

Finally, Immie pulled away and looked at Misha with eyes that held weariness and fatigue, eyes that had learned to mistrust. Then she whispered in Misha's ear, "Let's go home now."

Misha drove them back home to Oakland. They crawled into bed, and Immie rested her head against Misha's chest. It was the first time Misha felt like she could inhale.

Immie's breath grew even, and before long, she was still. Misha smoothed her hair and held her tight. She then stayed awake for hours, holding and pretending to protect her lover from all sorts of imaginary evils. Like Peter Pan playing the brave fellow in need of a mother, Misha was a scared woman determined to protect her soulmate. Maybe if she could imagine 3000 impossible situations and think about saving Immie, then someday when and if they became ready to talk about their sick marriage, Misha could use all of these imagined successes to fight to save them one more time—for real. After she imagined killing a dragon and fifty ninjas, she finally drifted off.

The morning found Misha, and she discovered that she was alone in bed. Groggily, she rolled over and picked up her cell phone. There were new messages from the dating app and one from Immie: "I need some space for me. Why don't you go and visit Jeff? I think it will be better for both of us."

CHAPTER 2

THAT NIGHT IN THE BAR was the last time Misha would see Immie for a long while. She texted her over and over but only got a few vague replies—about "making things easier" and "needing space." She didn't come home for so much as a change of clothes. After a couple of days, Misha gave in and booked a flight to visit her best friend, Jeff Martin, in Washington, D.C.

She didn't want to leave, but as there seemed little alternative, she decided she'd enjoy it. She'd never admit it aloud, but this was easy to do. Jeff made the world exciting and crazy. Misha loved his ability to turn life into an adventure.

Now all that stood between Misha and that adventure was the Reagan Airport in D.C. Airports had always made Misha happy. It was a joy from childhood. She disembarked, watching travelers pass by and remembering when she'd spend all day making signs in preparation for a visiting relative or a family friend. Back in those days, before 9/11, going to the airport had been something special. She sighed at the thought of those magical days ending because the TSA had only gotten more powerful and invasive, even with a track record of being mostly useless at catching bad guys. However, they were adept at intimidating innocent Muslims, people of color, and mothers who dared to provide food for their babies. A world devoid of welcome posters and filled with increased fear—Misha wondered how this could be better for humanity.

The people in front of Misha as she slowly worked her way to the terminal exit shuffled along, looking confused and half mad. Small items hung from them like Skeksis from Jim Henson's *The Dark Crystal*: a pillow around the neck… headphones. And luggage and bags covered them until only their faces showed under hoodies. Perhaps that's what happens to humans when they're in limbo: they cling to things. Not Misha, though. When she flew, she handed herself over to the nascent state between human with responsibilities and human starting a journey of discovery and hoping for a USB charging port. A part of her refused to let go of the dream created in changing locations. The activity was transformative in providing new perspectives—if a person was willing to accept the challenge.

There was no point in thinking about Immie and her delicate hands, which were so strong at breaking Misha's heart through typed words. It was hard for Misha to admit that Immie was right, as always. Nothing had changed, and currently, there was nothing else to do. Immie was hurting, and Misha was hurt. Conversations only seemed to add fire to their pain. So Misha hoped that time apart would make the heart grow fonder or help her gain the strength to lose this last important thing, her love. Nearly at the exit point, Misha breathed deeply, moving all the pains in her heart and head to the very back of her mind. It was time to focus on what was about to happen and what she could control.

Washington, D.C. has never had a reputation for being the friendliest or prettiest city, but it did have the distinction of being Jeff's home, and as such, it was the most perfect city in the world to Misha. A best friend was essential. Misha couldn't stop herself from giggling with excitement as she saw his steely gray eyes and the slight stubble that added a touch of rough to his otherwise immaculate appearance. He stood out among the flustered relatives and drivers holding signs like beacons.

Crossing the line of demarcation between purgatory and the land of the living (as defined by the TSA), Misha jumped into a Jeff hug that was warm and welcoming. She could feel the scratchy wool of his suit and smell a cologne that was three parts sexy and one part sweet fresh tobacco. Misha wondered if it was the Alan Cumming cologne she got him for Christmas last year. She grinned at the thought of it smelling so amazing on him.

"Does it ever get annoying being so damn perfect?" Misha whispered in Jeff's ear as she held onto his solid frame. He had to hug her the whole time. She demanded it. Jeff thrived on Misha's demanding love. It made him feel needed.

"I'll let you know if I ever bother to commit to perfection. But who has the time when there are so many wonderfully imperfect things I've yet to do?" He kissed her cheek. "Here, take this and go change." He handed her a dress bag. "I'll get your suitcase. Is it the one with duct tape on it?"

"Yep, the tape with the mustache print. It'll go so well with your suit."

Jeff often joked about Misha's kitsch taste. It amused him that she was so beautiful but would surround herself with such odd choices. "Indeed." His face registered disgust, but his eyes laughed.

Misha was intrigued by what might be in the bag. Once, he surprised her by arranging an afternoon of skydiving over the Pacific coast, followed by a picnic on the beach. Or there was the time he took her to a minor celebrity's party, and she got to see the celebrity's real talent—one fit for X-rated movies. Whatever Jeff had planned, it was going to be epic.

Inside the tight confines of the airport bathroom, Misha

unzipped the bag with excitement. *Oh my god, it's a party dress, but more for cock than cocktails. Latex. How the actual fuck am I supposed to put on a latex dress in this bathroom? Oh, excellent, there's lube in here too. Who doesn't love clothes that require a lubricant to get them on? Thanks, Jeff.* Out of the bag came a black bodice that flared at the skirt, a bottle of lubricant for putting on said dress, slightly platformed Mary Janes, and a high-end flared trench coat. *Where on earth can we go with me wearing this sort of thing?*

After much grunting, muttering, and praying, Misha left the bathroom, looking very professional in her trench coat. Maybe it was the vague smell of latex, the feeling of oil against her skin, or all the pressure of the dress, but she was starting to feel naughty and curious about where this was heading.

"We have been hearing you are keeping secrets, and I am here to make sure you talk," Misha whispered into Jeff's ear as she came up behind him. She tried to do a Russian accent, but it fell somewhere between American and French. It was shameless and tacky, just like the dress and the way she pressed her breasts into Jeff's back. She felt his body tense up for a moment, but then he turned around and his face was the same mask of welcoming mischief.

"You look nice in that coat, but it's good weather today, so why don't you take it off?" Jeff's eyes twinkled.

He's in a playful mood, and I like it. "You do remember I'm a homebody nowadays, but it sure is fun to play dress up. Shall we get ice cream and call it a night?" Misha attempted to bring herself and her friend back to their senses.

"Sweetie, it's like giving a blowjob in handcuffs: you never really forget the technique." He eyed Misha up and down in the least subtle way possible.

"You are a horrible perv." Misha took in a deep breath.

Flirting can be so much fun. Why couldn't every day be filled with shameless ego-feeding flirting?

"Takes one to know one. I saw you eyeing me as you came out of the terminal."

Busted. "So, where are we going with me in this attire?"

"Wouldn't you like to know." Jeff did have a plan. It was against protocol to take Misha, but he figured the boss would forgive him this once. No-one could have planned around two competing missions, so he decided the most elegant solution was to use one to achieve the other. As long as he did it flawlessly, no-one would care. And Jeff was always flawless.

That evening, Jeff took them to a dark quarter of the city where a few homes shared space with warehouses and auto shops. They walked along a silent street to a one-story warehouse with a blue light shining on a sign over the door that read "The Quandry." Misha thought it was the best name for a business in D.C., where everything seemed difficult and uncertain.

In a dark lobby, Jeff took Misha's coat. He led her by the hand down some stairs and into a space that looked like a church basement, except for the "unusual" furniture along the walls, and decrepit cheap tables and chairs around the middle of the room. Jeff led Misha to a table. In front of them, a flogging was taking place. Loudly. It had been a long time since Misha had been in a situation like this, and she sat uncomfortably, trying to remember how to behave. For the last ten years, an exciting night consisted of work dinners and then home to pajamas and snuggles on the couch as she and Immie Netflixed and chilled. The Quandry was a million miles from that. Misha felt alone and apprehensive on the one hand and excited on the other.

Over the noise, Misha said, "I don't remember what to do in a place like this."

"The rules here can be summed up like this: 'Don't be a dick and everything will go fine.'"

"Jeff… maybe you've forgotten, but it was this sort of thing that got me into all this trouble with Immie in the first place. I don't think I want to be here." Misha's voice was edgy, but her eyes didn't move from the performance. Despite her protest, something inside her was waking up. Yes, she regretted that her sexually adventurous younger self became the target of an ex-lover in a tell-all book, but this world had once made her feel so alive and accepted. Kinksters had a habit of being welcoming and had once helped her find herself. Maybe she could fit in again. Was that why Jeff had brought her here?

"No, my love, this isn't what got you into your current predicament. A million things led to this, and not one of them was your fault. I've seen you cut yourself into smaller and smaller pieces over the last year. You've stopped being yourself, and there's no Misha left. Tonight, we're going to be irresponsible, and nothing terrible will happen. You need to allow yourself to be all of Misha again. She's an amazing person." Jeff's forceful but protective expression scared Misha. The scolding had its intended effect.

Jeff turned to watch the performance again. He couldn't tell her everything he knew about why that book was written and published: she couldn't handle the full truth in her fragile, self-loathing state. Jeff would get revenge for Misha, just not today. The fights with Immie had nothing to do with Misha either, but that was going to be harder to fix. Jeff was hell bent on bringing his friend back from near extinction, but it would take time and a plan. Unfortunately, tonight, he needed her as window dressing while he tied up another problem.

Misha found herself syncing her breath with the man on the Saint Andrew's cross. It was almost meditative. "I appreciate that this place is called The Quandry and all, but I wish it were called

'Mitch McConnell.' Think about it: 'I saw Mitch McConnell filled with kinksters last night. I blew a load in Mitch McConnell last night. The options are endless.'"

Jeff saw through her need to use humor to deflect from her discomfort. His "uh-huh" response silenced her. She wondered why she'd come across the country to be stonewalled and shamed for being passably funny. She was considering calling an Uber. This wasn't her scene. These weren't her people anymore. But she was here and dressed for the night so decided to give it five more minutes and see if things improved.

"See that guy over there?" Jeff asked, without shifting his gaze. "I've played with him here before. He loves a proper spanking. If you can persuade him to let you spank him, I'll do anything you want for the rest of the night." He looked meaningfully into her eyes with a smoldering look that said "anything" was up to her discretion. The ball was now in her court. It was a Thursday night in D.C., and she was never going to see any of these people again.

Jeff felt his phone vibrating in his pocket. The source would be upstairs in a few minutes. He needed this pass to go as planned. He had to talk with the ambassador's assistant without the officer or Misha tagging along.

"Challenge accepted. Any other instructions, Captain?"

"None."

Jeff was starting to look bored, something that always drove Misha to do the brashest things. She stood up and strutted over to the man in the slightly wrinkled suit at the table on the far left. There was enough sass in her step to ensure he couldn't focus on anything else.

With only the table between them, she bent forward, palms resting on the tabletop. "May I sit with you?"

"You can, but I'm not going to talk to you. I'm not here to... I'm just..." He looked at his hands, folded on the table.

He hated it when he got sent on jobs like this, full of rich and powerful people doing weird shit. He realized he'd been watching this woman and would now have to get her out of his line of sight. Something was going down in this room tonight, and he had to catch it.

"I think you will." Misha was starting to feel her old self again. This guy was a nobody, so why not play a little rough?

"What makes you think that?" His gaze followed her arms and up to her face.

"Well, for one, you can see my tits, and I have fantastic tits. Sure, you might say that you're gay or not that into whatever, but you, my friend, were born of a woman, and as such, you have certain universal ingrained interests, like appreciating life-giving, open-24-hours breasts. Tell me I'm wrong." Misha was taken back a bit by her own words. It was hard to keep a straight face. But it was something to focus on that didn't involve Immie.

The man's eyes moved from Misha's face to her breasts. He caught himself and looked back down at the table. "You're not wrong," he said to the table.

"Exactly. So now I'm going to tell you something else. I came out in this dress to have a special time tonight, and there aren't that many people here. I suspect you're a gentleman. I need you to do something to pick up my evening. You're in a unique position to save the day."

"Am I?" He was smiling now at the table and sighed. Meeting a woman like this was the sort of thing that happened in movies, not in some grungy bar in D.C. Elliot couldn't believe his luck. He scanned the nearly empty room and decided it was okay if he carried on this conversation for a few minutes. He'd get back to work when there was someone to observe. Until then, he'd blend in with this woman, who did have unbelievably sexy breasts.

"I need you to go lay over that horse thing over there, drop your pants, and let me give you a proper spanking." Misha was encouraged by the fact that this man was now eye-fucking her breasts.

"Um, actually, I'm here to meet someone. Otherwise, I'd be inclined to do as you say. I don't think I've ever met anyone as persuasive as you before." He laughed and sat back in his chair, looking her up and down.

"Is your someone here yet?" Misha observed that he'd spread his knees while sitting back. Perhaps his pants were getting restrictive? Misha turned and scanned the room but found no-one there aside from the staff. The couple on the mainstage had left. Even Jeff seemed to have disappeared.

"No."

"Well, let me help you warm up for their arrival. Just a little paddling between new friends. I'm Sarah, by the way." Misha reached out her hand.

Elliot took it, laughed, and told her his name. He looked down at his wristwatch. "Ten minutes?" He couldn't maintain his cover if he blew off the only person in the room. All his training said he needed to blend in, so he had to say "yes."

"You won't regret it, Elliot. Let's go with 'please, more' as your safe word," Misha teased. She added, "'red' if it's too much for you." She took his hand and led him to the rocking horse.

As a staff member provided Misha with a table of accoutrements to choose from, Misha was reminded of the pistols offered at a duel. She took her time choosing. Elliot looked around the room and slowly lowered his pants, revealing boxer briefs and strong leg muscles. *Definitely a cyclist.*

Misha arched an eyebrow and began to instruct Elliot on the basics of etiquette—the little things, like saying "Thank you, Mistress" after each slap. *Shit, I forgot how much I missed this.*

Misha smiled as she watched a nervous Elliot take his place across the horse.

"Five," Misha announced, a second before the crop landed on Elliot's ass.

"Thank you, Mistress." Elliot's voice struggled to stay level.

The muscles in his thighs tensed in a way that Misha found attractive. She laid off the pressure on the second strike. She could see that he wasn't about to back down. It was up to her to control the situation and to get him to the other side, titillated and wanting more. This type of person was her favorite: he had to follow everything through to the logical conclusion. She was only too happy to oblige as she measured out the following strikes.

"One." Misha moved her body so she could talk directly into his ear, making the space between them more intimate. "I always keep my promises, so I'll let you go now. But if you had given me the time, I would have had you doing things you would enjoy 'regretting' tomorrow. Thanks for playing." She patted his bottom.

His eyes had the gloss of someone who'd slipped into another world, unsure of why he was there and why he was leaving. "I understand…. Thanks." He pulled up his pants and wandered to his table. He scanned the room, and not finding his companion, he resumed looking at his hands.

To Misha, he looked like an actor at his mark on the stage, waiting for another actor to join him and start the scene. Surprisingly, this image made her sad. Then she realized he looked ashamed and beaten. Just as she'd felt when she deplaned that afternoon, defeated, embarrassed, and waiting for something that wasn't coming back. She promised herself that it was time to stop waiting to live.

She sauntered back upstairs and asked the man at the desk if there was somewhere to smoke. He gave her a few complicated directions, and after going through a maze of turns, she reached a hidden patio. And there was Jeff, chatting up some good-looking young man. Typical. Jeff hadn't given up smoking like he said he had, and this man was exactly his type. Even in a nearly empty bar, Jeff could find a smolderingly attractive man. Misha approached and leaned her shoulder against Jeff's, smiling at the other guy. He smiled back, but then straightaway stood up and left.

"Sorry, Misha, but I thought you might be a while. I see by your face that you've won the wager. Shall I take you home?" The worry lines around Jeff's face had softened into a placid expression. The asset had been able to share the required information without interruption from the cops or other agents, and he should be able to get that info out tomorrow. One situation handled. Now what to do with Misha?

Smiling, Misha said, "Maybe we play just a little bit first? Old times' sake and all of that."

Jeff laughed and put out his cigarette. He had the expression of one who's fated to give in to the will of another forever.

CHAPTER 3

MISHA SAT AT A QUARTZ kitchen bar, cradling a cup of coffee in one hand and her cell phone in the other. She was in Jeff's semi-detached brick house in the historic West Village. There was one text from Immie, which Misha read over and over: "Should I reschedule the meeting with the contractor on the 10th?"

What does that mean? Does she want me to come back, or does she want to cancel? Maybe I don't answer. I'll look at some other texts. But what contractor? I'm in so much trouble…

"Morning," Jeff said, half asleep, walking straight to the coffee pot. He walked with a bit of a limp, but he was sure it wasn't bad enough for anyone to notice and ask him what the matter was when he went out. Which was good, because what he did alone with his best friend wasn't suitable for public consumption. With a grin, he imagined the clutching of pearls if he told them the cause.

"Good morning," Misha replied in a sing-song, placing her phone face down on the counter.

"Well, it's obvious you're pleased with yourself." He poured a black coffee and sat gingerly at the counter, resting one hand on her knee. He was relieved to see that she had some of her glow back.

"Is it?" Misha nearly sighed but giggled instead. It was hard being mentally in two places at once. There was no point in bringing Jeff into her mess of a relationship, especially when she'd already promised herself a mental break from the heartache.

"Yes, but it's good. You need to have a little fun. I'm sorry you lost your job, but it was only a job, and it was ages ago. There'll be others. It's time to get back on the horse. You must be driving Immie up the wall, staying at home every day." Moments of direct sincerity like this between the friends weren't rare, but they were always significant. Jeff shifted his gaze to the phone on the counter. "How's Immie today?"

"Not up yet." The answer maybe came out too fast. Immie wasn't something Misha wanted to discuss today… or any other day.

"Don't fuck it up with Luna." Jeff had always insisted that Immie was the mortal version of Luna Lovegood from *Harry Potter*. It certainly helped his case that Immie was an astronomer and a platinum blonde. Jeff felt that although things were strained between the pair, they'd work it out, one way or another. "You lucked out with that one."

"You're correct." Misha couldn't stop her sigh now. She picked up the phone and scrolled through photos of Immie. Hundreds of them. Enough for a whole afternoon of self-indulgent whining and fantasizing.

"Right. So when are you going to get a new job?"

"Jeff, I'm blackballed from universities. Every application I've sent has been rejected. And Immie loves the lab at Berkeley. She isn't going to move. She's made that clear." Misha frowned over the photo of herself and Immie at the Mauna Kea Observatory on their last vacation.

Jeff knew that look. Misha needed to let go of the past before it killed her, and if last night was any indication, he had an idea how to help. "Listen, Misha…"

Misha put the phone down. She could indulge her sadness when her friend wasn't around.

Looking down at his coffee cup, Jeff said, "I need to tell you something about last night."

Misha breathed in slowly. *Does he regret it, and am I going to shrink right back down to nothing? Please let me have this. Let last night be fun.* She fought the urge to run from the room before he could say anything more.

"Something happened…" Jeff could see her discomfort, but he had to speak to keep her safe and to see how capable she was going to be in navigating difficult situations.

Fuck, it's going to be awful. But he seemed so into it at the time. Okay, I'll brace myself, and we'll deal with it. Far better than having a novel published about me eight years from now—fucking Ryan.

"So, the guy I asked you to go and talk with last night… I know him, sort of. He's a federal officer." Jeff rushed through the second sentence and then looked at Misha, preparing for her reaction.

"I thought you were going to say you regretted last night." Misha took a relieved breath. "Did you say Elliot is a fed?"

Jeff seemed unconcerned and leaned back in his chair. "He and I don't know each other well, but he was looking for someone last night. I needed to meet with that person and for them to be able to slip in and out without Elliot seeing either of us together. You participated unknowingly in a very minor setback in a larger federal investigation."

"What? I just interrupted a federal investigation. What does that mean? Did I break the law?" Misha tried to reconcile the image of Elliot in his boxer briefs leaned over the spanking horse with Elliot in a suit arresting her for obstruction of justice. The only part of the two images that could overlap would be a gratuitous use of handcuffs.

"You didn't interrupt a federal investigation—just delayed it a little. Better than I expected. You're good at getting people to do whatever you want. Do you know that?" Jeff smiled. He'd dropped the bomb, and the fallout wasn't half as bad as he'd anticipated.

"What are you trying to tell me? That guy, Elliot: you never played with him before? Instead, you lied to me, hoping I'd distract him while you…. Is that why you disappeared?" Misha would admit that being naughty is something she enjoyed, but she was still a law and order kind of person. Her idea of rebelling against the law was jaywalking. Obstructing the police in the course of their duty was not okay. But she hadn't known he was a police officer, and he did give his consent…

"Calm down. It's not that big a deal. I needed you to distract the good officer so I could get out of the room more or less undetected. You did great. Thank you. I accomplished what I needed to do. I appreciate your help, and when you're hanging out around town over the next couple of days, I'd advise you to avoid talking to strangers about me. If you're in a situation where you feel it's necessary to talk about me, please say that we're old friends and that I'm a linguistics professor at Georgetown. That's more than enough information to explain what you're doing in D.C." The more confused and irritated Misha got, the calmer Jeff felt. As he spoke, he found himself re-centering in his cover. There was no reason that cover couldn't protect Misha like it had protected him all these years. But he realized he'd need to be more thoughtful in his word choice from now on if he didn't want Misha to have a panic attack.

"But we *are* old friends, and you *are* a professor at

Georgetown?" Misha was very confused, and her fingers started writing away on the bar: "friend," "Georgetown," "professor".... Suddenly there was a question in her mind—had she missed something about her friend?

Sometimes, Jeff couldn't help himself. Egging on his newly paranoid friend was a bit of fun, so he said, "Again, if possible, avoid talking to strangers, especially if you run into that officer again. If anything, focus on how much he liked his spanking." The last bit Jeff savored, a twinkle in his eye taking over as he imagined Misha beating the unsuspecting officer. Some days, knowing Misha was the best. If she were just slightly less well-behaved, they'd be unstoppable.

"How do you know I spanked him? You weren't even there." Misha could tell Jeff was teasing her now and wasn't sure if everything he was saying was a joke or if there was some truth to it. He could get like this sometimes, being so obtuse that it was hard to tell. Years ago, she tried to learn more about his life before they'd met. He talked in the same way as now, interjecting scary possibilities and then pivoting to flirtation, as if she'd forget her questions. After hours of this Alice in Wonderland conversation, all she'd learned was that Jeff was originally from somewhere in Upstate New York and that he had a mom and a dad. So she gave up.

"I drink, and I know things," Jeff said, leaning back and feeling fully in control of the situation again.

"Slow your roll, Tyrion Lannister. It sounds like my night was far more complicated than I realized, and I'd appreciate if you'd tell me about it." Misha doubted the direct route would work, but it was worth one last try.

"Okay…" Jeff considered his words and what would be the right amount of truth for this situation. "I needed to talk to someone discreetly, and I needed a distraction. I knew you could do with a night out to escape the funk you've been in, so I decided to kill two birds with one stone. I planned to have you provide a visual distraction for two minutes of conversation, but you got him to do quite a lot more, you minx. You persuaded a federal officer to blow off his job to be beaten by you. That's a marketable skillset, my friend. Have you considered pursuing it as a job?"

"Don't flatter me. No-one would pay me to spank them."

"I think you're wrong, and I imagine the pay in San Francisco would be impressive."

Misha rolled her eyes.

Jeff shrugged and continued, "I was able to talk to the guy you saw me smoking with and get what I needed, in private. I appreciate your help, but Elliot might be a bit miffed about his amateur-hour behavior and want to know what happened while he was distracted. So, Officer Elliot may look for you as a target for his mistakes. If he does, know that I didn't do anything illegal, and neither did you. The conversation we had isn't relevant to government or police activity, though the young man's sexual orientation is a target for those who wish to use him as an asset. Please do me the favor of saying we're old friends, and I took you out for a night of amusing debauchery, if, and only if, anyone asks." Jeff felt beyond pleased with himself now. He'd managed to frame the evening, stroke his friend's ego, and bring in sexual orientation discrimination—that would be plenty to get Misha on his side.

"So, you're telling me you know this Elliot guy, but you didn't know spankings were his thing? You sent me over to get turned down?" Misha considered the picture Jeff was painting and was shocked that she'd managed to pull it off.

"I said I know *of* him. I only know him by reputation. The rest you said is correct, and I was going to make it up to you.

I mean, I think we both know that I made it up to you." A Cheshire-cat grin broke out across Jeff's face.

"So, what were you doing, if it wasn't to interfere with a police investigation? Why did you need to talk to that guy? Are you doing something bad? Are you in trouble?"

"I'm not going to discuss that part because it's extremely private and not illegal. It's personal," Jeff replied curtly and got up to refill his coffee.

"Excuse me, I may or may not have broken the law, and I don't deserve to know why?" Misha was building up again to a full case of self-indulgent indignation.

"You didn't break the law. I was doing my job, which isn't illegal by any means or definitions."

What aren't you telling me, Jeff? There's a reason you're being cryptic, and it's deeply frustrating.

Jeff continued, "It's going to be fine. D.C. is a weird town. There are always at least three layers to everything you see going on around you. It's a cat-and-mouse place, and no-one knows which one they are—often, everyone is both. Be careful." He was glad that he gave her this advice. It would serve her well for a long time.

"Okay. Fine." Misha stopped spelling the conversation out on the counter and moved onto a more enjoyable discussion. "So, I was thinking the Natural History Smithsonian today and then drinks—"

"Fuck off. I hate that shit. Except for Air and Space, but we'll do that tomorrow. I'm going to take you to Georgetown and ask you to pick something up for me over at Georgetown Park. You can find your way over to the Smithsonian from there." Jeff detested being in places full of tourists and sticky, poorly behaved children. Why would Misha even suggest such an activity?

"Feels like I ought to be going to the Spy Museum instead. You're acting very cloak and dagger right now."

"Enjoy the excitement, Darling. Power can be intoxicating." He shifted a bit uncomfortably in his seat, exaggerating the state she'd left him in. It'd be pointless for her to deny that she enjoyed having total control over things, people, situations.

"Fine. Where am I going, and what am I picking up? Promise me it isn't another distraction?" Misha didn't know why she asked for this promise: she was leaning toward believing Jeff was making all this up to make her feel more important than she was. More likely, Jeff went off to find his next Mr. Right, and all of this was a story he was telling to entertain himself.

"I'd like you to go to a place called HMH Tobacconist to pick up a lighter I'm getting engraved. Ask for Max to show you his novelty pipe collection while you're there. That guy's quite a character. Right. Let's get going."

Jeff hustled Misha through the getting-ready routine and out the door, as if they were late for an important event. She trusted Jeff a little less now and found herself a little less concerned too. She already knew she'd help out her friend with no expectation of getting any answers, but she also knew she'd take her time doing it. She was pissed that after what he'd gotten her to do unknowingly (if he wasn't teasing, that is), he still couldn't be bothered to spend the day with her. Well, at least he didn't ask her to help him bury a body.

CHAPTER 4

JEFF DROVE MISHA TO HIS office on campus. After a quick tour of his labs, showing Misha his team's newest toys and gadgets, he left her back at the office and rushed out for a meeting downtown. Misha hung out for a while, skimming through books off the shelf, hoping the bone-chilling wind would die down before she went for cupcakes, coffee, and Jeff's lighter. It was only a mile to the posh shopping district, but she was used to the mid-coastal California weather, where even the cold winds that blew through the streets of San Francisco seemed positively balmy compared to these early spring days in D.C.

The quietness of the room soon made her mind wander. After nearly two years of searching, she feared that she'd never get to be a professor again. Every week, she sent out applications to U.S. colleges and universities. She'd also begun applying abroad, even though Immie had made it clear she preferred to stay in Berkeley. Misha's mind swirled at the prospect of never working again and of losing Immie: both felt likely and terrifying. Her life was quickly disintegrating.

To try and stop these thoughts, Misha braved the cold and got on with her tasks. As she walked along, with eyes watering and nose running, she tried to take in the beautiful churches and charming shops. Every half block, welcoming cafés, shops, and other warm places were calling her.

Then she saw a man marching up the street in her direction. It was Elliot.

"Hello, *Sarah*." He stopped just a foot away.

"No bicycle?" Misha asked, her mind feeding her the image of his muscular thighs.

"Why didn't you tell me who you are, Ms. Campbell?"

Despite her surprise, Misha realized that this meeting was just too convenient. It must be some sort of practical joke Jeff was playing on her. How else would Elliot know her name?

"I don't know what you're talking about."

"Why did you give me a fake name last night?" His look was contemptuous.

Was he really confused about why a woman would give a fake name to a man she'd just met in a club like that?

"You work for Jeff Martin," he growled.

"I don't work for anyone." Misha's teeth were chattering. Standing in the crosswind was worse than walking through it.

"Did he make you talk to me? What did he tell you about me?" Elliot was getting more and more angry.

Misha realized this wasn't a joke after all. "I don't understand what you want or who you are, but you're obviously upset, so why don't we go get a cup of coffee or something?" she said, attempting to soothe him.

"I don't want to go anywhere with you. Answer my questions."

"I'm freezing. You're just a guy I met yesterday and had no intention of seeing again, but you're yelling at me on the street." Misha reached out a hand to gently touch his elbow, but he yanked his arm back. She realized that if she was going to get him to calm down, she'd have to change tack. "Okay, Jeff Martin is a friend. You must have seen us at the table together?"

"No, I didn't." Elliot's posture and facial expression changed. Misha felt something had shifted inside him. "Did Jeff tell you to do *that* to me?"

"No," Misha lied. "You were just staring down at the table and looking sad. I thought it would cheer us both up. I don't understand why you're upset, and you're starting to really scare me. What's going on?"

Elliot looked like all his muscles had contracted. He pulled his badge out of his pocket and showed it to Misha.

The tears in Misha's eyes and the chattering of her teeth weren't solely due to the cold anymore. This man was ballistic. She wanted to get away from him as quickly as possible, but she wasn't sure if she could walk away from an officer.

"I can ask you here, or I can arrest you: what are you doing with Jeff Martin?"

Misha didn't know what to say. She'd already misrepresented the truth a bit. She opted for a show of defiance. "I don't like threats. I told you I was out with my friend. We were sitting at the same table when I left to talk to you. I don't know what your problem is, but I can tell you I did nothing wrong."

"We'll see about that."

Misha backed up a couple of steps to create some space between them. "Does Jeff know about your personal life? Are you an ex-boyfriend or something?"

"No. If someone's told you I'm a fag, it's a lie."

Elliot looked around, as if someone was watching them. Misha wished that was the case. She had to get out of this conversation before he attempted to detain her. The last thing she needed in her life right now was an arrest record. How would she explain that to Immie? But there again, would it even matter to Immie anymore?

"You're threatening me on the street and using offensive slurs. Give me your badge number. Let's call and confirm that you have authority to question me."

This seemed to do the trick. "Tell your friend," Elliot said, "I have my eye on him and all of his associates. I'll take you all down if you get in my way again."

Misha understood that the conversation was over. "Got it."

She walked around Elliot and rushed down the street. He shouted her name, but she kept walking. Then he shouted again, this time calling her a bitch. She turned around and saw he was following her.

"Remember, get in my way again, and you'll regret it. I know all about you, Misha Campbell." He flipped her off and turned down a side road.

Misha's heart was racing. She walked as fast as she could. Crossing M Street, she thought she saw Jeff walking away from her, but that couldn't be possible, since he was at a meeting downtown. She wished it had been him though, to protect her in case that crazy man returned.

She was relieved when she finally reached the cupcake shop. She thought about how D.C. was a city of extremes—when it was good, it was great, but when it was hard, it could be so cold and scary. After she'd been served, it took her quite a while to calm down enough to brave leaving the shop.

When she eventually reached HMH Tobacconist, Misha was absorbed by its oddity. Surrounded by fancy upscale establishments, it was such a strange little shop. Pipes and chessboards of various value and every sundry in between filled the small glass-enclosed cupboards. She stopped in front of a wall of hookahs, imagining someone trying to sell her one. *Who would buy that hookah? The standard bowl means that shit is going to end up in your water. What you need is a hookah with a filter, so your water stays as clean as your soul. Well, not your soul Misha, but other people's—you know, people who don't interrupt federal investigations into potential crimes against the state that your best friend may or may not be part of. Fuck, what have I done?*

Misha laughed and made her way over to the clerk busying himself at a desk. "Excuse me. I need to pick up a lighter for a friend."

"Go choose it and bring it to the counter." The clerk didn't look up.

"I was told it's been put aside. It's for Mr. Martin."

The clerk still didn't look up. "I'll need to go in the back to check." He set his pen down, then picked it up again and began tapping some boxes on his desk.

Misha wasn't going to stand there waiting like a fool, so she wandered off to have another look around the store. As she was examining some chessboards, she saw him finally leave the counter. She didn't enjoy playing chess but loved the idea of it.

The clerk had been gone about ten minutes, during which time a couple of people had entered the store but left when there was no-one to help them. Misha got the impression that the clerk wasn't interested in doing his job. Finally, he re-emerged, and Misha went up to his desk. Again, he didn't look up. She cleared her throat. No response.

"Excuse me," she said.

"What?"

"The lighter?"

"We have Mr. Martin's package here."

"So, can I have it, please?" She didn't understand this guy at all.

Still looking down, he reached below the register and handed

Misha a package. She couldn't help but wonder if it had been there the whole time.

"Thank you. Also, my friend told me to look at the novelty pipe collection. Can you show it to me?"

The clerk stood up straight and looked at Misha like she was crazy. "No." His gaze moved from Misha to a spot on the wall above her left shoulder. Misha turned slightly and saw items stuffed into curios. She couldn't ascertain why he was staring at the wall. Then, suddenly, the clerk said, "I'll see if *he* is available. Give me a minute." He left.

Two minutes later, an older gentleman with silver-white hair emerged from what Misha assumed was the storeroom. This must be Max himself, with his Hawaiian shirt and his white mustache on an otherwise clean-shaven face. With a Jimmy Buffett energy mixed with drug-lord swagger, he seemed to take up the whole room. He looked around, as if seeing the place for the first time. After this survey, he settled his attention on Misha.

"Hello, my dear, you asked about my collection?" He took Misha's hand into both of his and kissed the back of it. He must have been quite the ladies' man when he was younger. He still had a palpable sexual presence. Misha felt a bit overcome. "A friend of Jeff's is a friend of mine, so I'll happily show you my collection. It's in the back. Please follow me." He scanned the room again before ushering Misha through the door.

The door didn't lead to a storeroom but to a corridor with more doors off to either side. After walking at a brisk pace, the man unlocked a door on the right and stood aside for Misha to enter. She wasn't sure why, but she felt a sudden dread about going into this room with a man she didn't know. She could hardly turn and run though, so she walked inside.

It was a large room and opposite in every way to the store itself. Whereas the store held random items without any unifying theme, this room was like a 19th-century European study, fit for the aristocracy to sip brandy and discuss matters of importance. It was lit by what appeared to be heirloom Tiffany glass lamps. Two of the walls had bookshelves that started at the floor and went all the way to the ten-foot ceiling. There were a few drawers built into the shelves that looked like they should hold specimens or secret folios from a bygone age. In the center of the room was a large dark-wood table with claw feet and ornate golden inlay. Misha looked at the older man for some explanation, but he was already pulling something out of one of the shelf drawers.

"Go ahead and sit at the table. I'll be there momentarily."

"Thank you, Mr....?" .

He looked up. "Sorry. Everyone calls me Max."

"I'm Misha."

Max set down a sizeable wooden box on the table in front of Misha. Every side of the dark brown box was carved into scenes from the high seas. There were naval battles and mermaids and krakens. It looked like something she might see behind a barrier in a museum, not on a table in front of her.

"Misha, inside here, you'll see some classic pieces. I hope you're not disappointed." He unlatched and lifted the cover off the box. Inside were five smoking pipes, all made of some kind of white stone. Each one portrayed a figurehead from an old sailing ship. Max picked up one of a woman busting out of a corset, her hand above her eyes and looking into the distance.

Misha smiled—it's like the woman was dying to get to shore to find some action, the salty wench. Misha began to imagine stories about her and her adventures.

"This is my great-grandfather's pipe. He was a privateer. Do you know what that is?"

"Sure, pirates for governments."

Max studied Misha as she looked at the pipe. She was cautious with the object, without being timid, and her face showed a deep curiosity. Max liked that she seemed to be taking everything in. Jeff had told Max this morning that she was ready for the next step. That was why Jeff had suggested that Max meet with her to make the final decision.

"Who did your great-grandfather work for?" Misha asked.

"Whoever paid the best, my dear." Max gave a half smile.

Misha studied the pipe a little longer and handed it back. Old versions of pin-ups in the forms of pipes weren't her thing. Why would Jeff recommend them? It was very odd. And she knew that Max was watching her. Something here was off, but since she'd arrived in D.C., it had been one strange event after another: the club, the brush-off from Jeff, the deranged officer, the rude clerk. Nothing about the place felt normal.

Max passed her a second pipe, which showed a kraken wrapped around a human skull. "This is made from something called 'meerschaum,' which in this particular case was mined and carved in Turkey. The other one is ivory. Note how this one feels much cooler to the touch due to the composition of the minerals."

Not knowing how to respond to this impromptu geology lesson, Misha changed the subject. "You have a love for the sea. Don't you, Max?"

"I wouldn't say that I'm in love with the sea. I just have an appreciation for mysteries beyond my comprehension." He took the second pipe from her hands and rested it carefully on the molded velvet lining of the box.

Max and Misha studied each other. Misha was starting to consider the possibility that she was having a breakdown, and none of this was happening. And Max was concerned that Misha might remember him. They'd met twice previously, when she was a child. First, he appeared as her mom's old friend. At the time, Misha was only three, so it's unlikely she'd remember how he took her to the zoo and how much she enjoyed him imitating the animal noises. The second time was when she was ten, and he was the school psychologist carrying out achievement testing. But although they were such short exchanges and from so many years before, maybe her memory was even more photographic than the tests suggested. He had to move faster if he was going to finish his assessment before she could finish hers.

Max closed the lid and gestured to the armchairs. He waited for Misha to sit down and then took a chair a few feet away.

"How do you know Jeff?" he asked.

"We're old friends." Why was he asking her about Jeff? She'd been friends with him for nearly two decades, and yet in the last four hours, she'd been asked about the nature of their relationship twice. How well did Jeff know this man with the fascinating hippy-rock vibe and his King of England library behind a shop?

"What makes you friends? You don't seem the same type." He leaned back comfortably in his chair.

"I suppose we have mutual passions." This wasn't something Misha had thought about before.

"I can imagine. Jeff and I have been friends for a long time as well, and I've come to learn about a few of his 'passions,'" Max chuckled. But despite his smile, Max was trying to block out images of Jeff that he would have preferred never to have seen. "Tell me, Misha, what's something you're passionate about?" He felt more confident that this line of questioning would keep her focused on the things he wanted to discuss. Maybe he could see how she handled two more questions before he got her to leave.

"I'm not sure anymore. I was a professor, but it seems more and more likely that I'll never be one again. I don't know *who* I am anymore. Everything feels so hard." Misha started spelling on the arm of the leather chair in large, sloppy cursive letters.

Max was surprised that she was still doing what he'd taught

her when he was the school psychologist. She had dyslexia, and he told her it would help improve her spelling, but it also seemed to help her organize her thoughts. She was a clever girl, using every skill to full potential. "A professor—I can see that. You seem like someone who others respect, and I know Jeff holds you in high esteem. What will you do if you can't find another professorship?"

"Your guess is as good as mine." Misha laughed and shifted in her seat. She was starting to feel small and young in Max's presence. He seemed kind, but part of her feared that even he, a stranger, could see that she was a failure.

"Life has a funny way of working out. I once—" Max broke off, tilting his head to the side. Misha couldn't see that Max had a small hearing aid that allowed him to maintain contact with the clerk. The clerk told him that some police officer was sniffing around in the store. Max made a mental note that Misha's evasion techniques still needed some work.

"Misha, Dear, I'm going to have to cut our visit short, I'm afraid. Something has come up. Did Jonathan give you a package?"

"If you mean the clerk, yes, he gave me Jeff's lighter."

"I believe he handed you the wrong package. Please could you give it to me? I have the correct one over here." Max knew Jeff's assessment was going to be accurate, but it was nice getting to see his protégé up close. It might be the last time he ever saw her, but it was worth it to see the impressive person she'd become.

"Of course." Misha pulled the box out of her bag and handed it to Max. He returned to the wall drawers and pulled out an identical package. She put it in her bag.

"So sorry to rush you off, but alas, the time has come for me to get back to work. But before you go, will you permit a sentimental old man to give you a bit of advice?"

"Sure." Misha was wrapped up in the authority and kindness that Max exuded.

"It sounds like you're going through something not good right now, and that's unfortunate. I see an engaging person before me, and I'm so happy to have made your acquaintance. In my many years, I've often thought I knew how something was supposed to turn out, only to be thwarted. Don't give up hope. In the moment when all seems lost, something better will come along to replace it. Trust in yourself and know some forces are watching out for you—I know it." Max took her hand into his and kissed it.

For some reason, their meeting together felt important to Misha, and she was reluctant to leave. So, in an attempt to delay things, she said, "Why's the store called HMH Tobacconist?"

Max seemed to go somewhere else as he gripped her hand tightly, leading her to the door. Over his shoulder, he said, "It's an inside joke. Maybe I can explain it the next time we meet."

Why on earth would I ever see him again?

He led her down the corridor, further to the right. "Go to the end of this hall and out to the alley. Take it to the right and then pull up Google to get to the closest metro station. Okay?"

"Okay. Thanks."

"And, Dear, best to head straight to the museum. It's going to start raining within the hour." Max couldn't help himself from talking to her like she was his grandchild. Letting her leave felt like heartbreak. He'd never cared for anyone the way he'd cared for her.

Misha made it to the Smithsonian's National Gallery of Art before the rain began. Walking around slowly, she thought of the great art before her and of the strange encounters she'd had since arriving in D.C. There was no way she could understand the wheels that were in motion that forced her into this city. Elements in D.C. were moving her closer to a future that she wouldn't have chosen for herself. Some of the key players were convening at this very moment, while Misha was looking at John

Singleton Copley's *Watson and the Shark*. Misha read the plaque and thought about how the artist used the shark to symbolize Satan attempting to claim another soul. *If I were the swimmer, would I grab the rope, reach for the hands of the sailors, or swim into the open pit of the shark's hungry mouth and give in to the darkness that awaits?*

CHAPTER 5

ANYONE WHO WAS ANYONE IN politics would tell you that the power in the United States wasn't to be found on the floor of the Senate, or even at 1600 Pennsylvania Avenue—those places existed only as a demonstration of power. The U.S. government was mainly window dressing. Power was brokered in the back of certain restaurants or particular men's clubs frequented by senators and judges. But those were the political power day traders who only knew about a secondary form of control. The real center of power in the U.S. was concentrated in the subterranean arena of one building—more specifically, in thirteen rooms along a corridor in what looked like an underground bunker. People all over the city walked above the actual seat of American power, but only fifty or so knew about this corridor and its secret rooms underneath.

Those fifty people, referred to from here on as the "pantheon," walked this corridor when necessary and kept the secret vacuum sealed. No leaks ever surfaced. The members of the pantheon kept the corridor a secret because to share it would mean losing access to this seat of power, or death. All members of the pantheon held secondary, and sometimes tertiary, power in the pantomime above ground to glean access to intel from across the globe. With their connections to each other, they satiated their hunger for power by tipping the scales of business. These were people who didn't take their roles of puppet masters for granted. Instead, they relished being part of a chosen few who could make the world in their images.

Unfortunately, even at the top of the top, where power and autonomy were privileges, there were also duties and responsibilities, checks, and balances. None of the pantheon wanted to lose their piece of the pie to usurpers, so they delegated the roles and responsibilities. Each member was assigned a room, "A" to "M," where they'd meet when called and make decisions as required. This method had served the pantheon well since its inception in the 1950s.

No-one has ever seen them at work. People walk above the rooms, carrying out their business with no knowledge that their efforts to sway, to protest, to vote have always been in vain. People would be in awe of the grandeur of the pantheon's mechanisms to keep the world order. Imagine being able to stare agape at their brilliance and courage to protect their fellow humans. Think about all of the ways our society has improved over the last fifty to sixty years, and think that we have these fifty people to thank.

If it were possible to visit this place in June of 2020, one would have gone to Boardroom M, on the south end of the corridor. Like something left over from the '60s, the walls were the color of an avocado no-one would want to eat. The flooring was brown, although this wasn't its original color. Along the wall opposite the door was a wooden buffet with tumblers and liquor bottles. The most significant thing in the room was a massive dark-wood table with round, burnt-orange upholstered chairs. There was a silence that was complete and stifling.

The table was far too large for the space, making the room

feel very tight and confined. Wood of a similar hue to the table covered the walls, which were aging equally poorly. One of these walls had a whiteboard that seemed to be at least twenty years younger than every other object in the room.

This room looked like a place where significant decisions had been made by great men. But with their passing, it had fallen into disrepair. Like any graveyard, it had been taken over by time. If one looked closely, these men could be seen standing at the decanter, working their magic on the whiskey, giving it the flavor of regrets, as the ghosts of men's desires do. That was the beautiful thing about time and neglect: it always destroyed the deeds of men but gave back by imparting the flavor of their activities into oak barrels and ignored decanters.

Three people entered this tribute to the white-collar worker of yesteryear. Each followed behind the other at precisely three paces and then sat in their respective burnt-orange chairs at the end of the table furthermost from the whiteboard. They took their seats on either side of the conference table without saying a word. Their movements showed the control and precision of a well-rehearsed scene or dance. Any observer posing as the proverbial fly on the wall, stuck to the dust and muck of nearly sixty years, would have the perfect vantage point to take in the ageless custom.

The three actors on the stage of this decrepit meeting room were two men and one woman. Their outfits would have been impressive in the business world in the late 1980s to mid-'90s. Though their style wasn't as old as the room itself, it lent the whole scene a feeling of being profoundly outdated.

The woman handed out a Manila folder to each of the men. She placed one on the table in front of her and another at the head of the conference table, where no-one was sitting. One man looked at his watch and shook his head. They sat in silence, trying not to look at each other.

Eventually, the door opened in the stuffy room, and the three stood up. A man in military dress took the seat at the head of the table, and the others sat back down. All four then opened their folders to the first page.

"Samuel's Affair," the woman read from the header.

"What are the assets involved?" asked the man in military attire.

"Five agents, thirty-three contractors, two branches of the military, one CIA cell, two NSA officials who are unaware of each other, ten million in ordnance, intel worth roughly one hundred million," answered the man wearing glasses and a suit.

The other man picked up the thread. "The risks are the intel and lives but not high-level assets. The opportunity is the money to be made from the intel."

"What do you all think?" the military man asked, without looking at any of them. He hated this part of his job: it wasn't good form to reduce political and military actions to vague transactional terms. Much was lost when abstract ideas, like information, were given a monetary value and juxtaposed with human lives. However, this was the way wars were conducted now—it was supposedly more objective. At least he was in the room and had the power to stop things when they got out of hand.

The woman spoke. "We believe it's a go."

They all placed their sheet face down, flipped to the next page, and repeated the process. The folders each held twenty sheets, all with the same types of information and the same assessments discussed and reviewed. It would be hard to say what the value of the meeting was. If the attendees were able to discuss the process, there'd be four vastly different answers. That was why there were rules: to limit personal subjective realities from slowing down the critical objectives. So, they continued with what they'd been taught by their predecessors and what they'd someday show their replacements. There was a retelling of facts, the same question, "What do you all think?," and the same response: "We believe it's a go." Occasionally, there was a point of clarification, but actual discussion was actively discouraged. This meeting represented the pinnacle of pantheon culture: a call and response, then a flip of the page.

Methodically, the team processed the requests, as was their right and duty. Each kept the critical points in mind to make sure their actions facilitated the movement of the objective "above ground." At one point, the man without glasses got up and poured from the brown carafe two fingers into three tumblers and, from the clear carafe, three fingers into the fourth tumbler. He dispersed the drinks. The man without glasses liked this part of the routine: at least he had control over this step. They continued their work.

"The Thompson Report," the woman read from the fifteenth sheet.

"What are the assets involved?" asked the man in military attire, thinking *only five more to go.*

The man with glasses answered, "An undetermined number of agents, many of high value, overlap with CIA, overlap with NSA, overlap with FBI, POTUS, seven senators, two supreme court justices, fifteen contractors, all branches of the military, multiple conglomerates, fifteen celebrities, multiple heads of state…" He paused to buff out a smudge on his glasses. The others glared at him, trying to determine if he was taking a break or was done speaking. He was always doing stuff like that, and it held them up or inundated the process with ambiguity.

The man without glasses wanted to speak: "The risks are multiple, and there've been different determinations from both Boardroom A and Boardroom L."

"What do you all think?" the military man asked, without even noting the addition of conflicting pantheon opinions.

The woman answered quickly, "We believe it's a go."

The man with glasses and the man without looked up and considered the woman across the table. They'd noticed her change in tone and her speed in responding, but they just went back to their sheets and turned the page.

After the last sheet, the men each closed their folder, returned them to the woman, then walked out of the room, maintaining three paces between each other. Carol returned to her folder and scanned the pages again, mumbling the words to herself. Finally, she stood, walked to the door, and dropped the four folders in the chute to the left. Once outside Boardroom M, she could hear the steps of her Boardroom team in the distance. She set out to walk the hidden route to her exit, close to the Capitol.

CHAPTER 6

MISHA COULD SMELL THE FISHY, summer air wafting up from the Danube and into Mr. X's apartment. She'd ended up here again. It had turned out her first mission for the CIA was more simple than anyone could have expected. She was tasked with turning Mr. X, a U.S. Embassy employee, into an asset, as the CIA determined if his family was operating with unfriendlies in the Russian government. It sounded both impressive and daunting to Misha, as she'd just completed at the Farm what was normally twelve months of training in only three. However, she was starting to trust the judgment of her superiors, as the mission was coming together in record time. Part of the success Misha attributed to the fact that Mr. X seemed to be the only American who'd read Thompson's tell-all and thought it was a rave review for Misha Campbell.

Mr. X had fallen all over himself to get to know Misha. He quickly fell into conversation with Misha when they "accidentally" met in front of the Embassy. By the end of that first conversation, he'd invited her to beers that weekend. She countered his beers with dinner and dancing. He stopped by Misha's desk two days later and gave her his cell number, leaving Misha no choice but to call him. Within a week, Misha had Mr. X on a short leash, both literally and figuratively.

To Misha's surprise, their relationship became sexual, although that wasn't expected or encouraged by her agency. Her reports to the office included accurate locations and intel, but she replaced the sexually explicit details with flirtatious overtures. Misha liked the heat between them and wasn't eager to give up something that felt this good. In the back of her mind, though, she wondered what would happen if anyone found out that she and Mr. X had far surpassed the activities covered in Mr. Thompson's book. Misha's superior at the agency was Jeff. This had surprised her a little, since they were such close friends, but maybe this provided her with extra coverage.

Mr. X had been starving to play from the second Misha walked in the door. In his excitement, he'd dirtied her favorite boots, but fortunately she'd anticipated this possibility and pre-treated them so there'd be no permanent stains. The enthusiasm and passion in the intimacy they created between them left both tired and hungry, so taking a break from their play, they retreated to the kitchen for refreshments.

"What do you want?" Mr. X asked.

Into Misha's mind there flashed an unwelcome image of Immie nestled against her chest. It had been too long since she'd seen her wife, let alone held her. The two had settled into a peaceful exchange of texts several times a week, but there was no intimacy in them.

Mr. X took the lack of an answer as confusion about the question, so he added, "Red or white?"

"Umm...." To rejoin the conversation, Misha tried to swim through her thoughts.

"I'm going to do us a favor and open the white. Both reds are the already-drunk kind. Do you mind?" Mr. X pulled out glasses and a corkscrew. With great aplomb, he then showed Misha the bottle and began to describe its qualities: "It's a bad year and a cheap white, but it goes down smooth." With that, he unscrewed the cork, threw it over his shoulder, and poured two glasses.

As he poured, Misha tried to focus on him and forget about Immie. "Does it taste of middle-class dreams that lead to other middle-class dreams? Not moving up in status but managing to finish college all the same?"

He chuckled but seemed surprised to hear his own laughter. He looked off down the hallway for a second, like he might have forgotten something back there, then replied, "No, slightly classier—as if your daughter was a stripper but married an accountant, so you feel accomplished as a parent."

"Oh, that's a good nondescript white. I usually only get the kind that tastes like the next day's hangover." Misha liked this the most about Mr. X: they talked of nothing and played off each other's jokes.

"I had one of those in the wine cupboard, too, but decided you should have the very best instead." He grinned at her and added, "Although whites are supposed to be chilled, sorry."

"Oh, you have a wine cupboard? You're awfully fancy. Growing up, we were so poor my mom had to keep her wine in a box in the fridge."

He shook his head in mock sadness. "That's awful, but at least cold. Next, you'll tell me you had to walk yourself to school without the nanny."

"I did, in high school. It was a rough life." They both smiled and took sips of their warm white wine.

As they stood around the butcher block, Misha looked at Mr. X. His bathrobe was mostly open, exposing a swimmer's chest. She then looked down at her outfit of black corset, fishnets, and black boots with a white smudge on the toe. She could feel ashamed, or she could feel sexy. She chose the latter.

"How much did Ryan mess up your life?" Mr. X asked suddenly.

"Ryan?" Misha pretended to be confused by the question.

"Ryan Thompson."

"Why are you bringing him up again?"

"I want to know who you are. We've been seeing each other these past few weeks, and I know everything about you without knowing you at all. I haven't met anyone like you before." His gaze didn't waver from her face. There was no judgment or anticipation. Misha felt like he was genuinely curious.

"I'm not *that* woman. Most of the stuff he wrote wasn't true, if that's what you're asking." Misha tried to smile. Her finger found a drop of wine and used it to trace "that" on the counter.

"I mean some of it was, I know," said Mr. X. "I also know Ryan. He's a classic dick who wants to own everything. But he was never one to retaliate—not at that level anyway. What happened?"

"You already know. I lost my job. I got a new one. Here I am." Misha was beginning to feel very uncomfortable. It was time to leave.

"And what's your job here: research assistant?"

"I'm blacklisted as a professor. I took what I could get, which was academic pity. Is this your go-to post-sex move, making your partner feel shitty?"

"Do you feel shitty?"

He hadn't acted this way once in their weeks together. Everything had been playful and light, but now he was changing the rules. Misha was trying to figure out the pivot of this change, to determine the effect on her purpose. If he knew more about her because of his relationship with Thompson, it might compromise the mission. Or was it time to offer him something to move the task to an end? He said he didn't like Thompson, and maybe he didn't like parts of his own family either, which would make it easier to gain him as an asset.

"I don't feel good about it. I liked Ryan Thompson once. If you know him, why don't you ask *him*? I don't know why he said those things." Misha opted to put the conversation back into Mr. X's court.

"I haven't talked to him since I was in college. The day I met you, it was clear that he misrepresented you, but you play close to the vest. I want to know who you are that you can drive a man to that."

"Oh, yeah. Why's that? Are you hoping for book material too?" Misha said with forced humor—anything to escape this uncomfortable territory.

"You try too hard."

"What?" She looked at him for a second and then went over to the open wine cupboard. She'd try and play the situation differently. She topped off her mostly full wine glass.

"You want something from me. Don't worry: your craft is solidly good, and I'm eager to learn what you want, but there's no rush. All of this has been very fun so far. Very." He eyed her with desire and added, "However, where I'm from, people always want something, so I'm very accustomed to *all* of the approaches."

"I see." Misha took a long drink from her glass.

"What I mean is, you're professional in your work, as well as something I don't see very often: compassionate. You're careful with people, but the woman in that book, she's evil. That was the woman I wanted to meet. I understand people like that, but I can't make sense of you. That makes you entirely alluring. So, talk. Tell me everything."

"I want you to tell me about your family's connections," Misha said, dropping her mission's objective into the conversation. It seemed he was aware of why she was really here, so what was the point in drawing this conversation out?

"Oh, they're connected in the most illegal and profitable ways." Mr. X refilled his now empty glass.

"Are you going to tell me more?" Misha felt like they were playing a game, and neither of them knew the rules.

"Probably not. I want to help you, Misha. I do. I hate my family more than I hate Thompson. However, they're the source of my income, and I have no desire to be cut off from the fountain of gold. But I can feed you some tidbits to keep the powers-that-be satisfied without raising too much trouble." He sighed and took a big gulp of wine.

"It's that easy?"

"It's that easy if I get what I want. I want to know you, and I want to help you. I like a project. I'll give you enough to push intelligence in the right direction to protect American interests, and my own, if you open up to me." He took his wine glass back to the living room.

Misha followed with her wine and sat on the couch next to him. He rested his hand casually on her knee. His body faced hers, but his head turned to look out the window.

"Tomorrow, we should go over to Bálna, the Whale. It's lovely over there. Have you been?" he asked.

"It's the glassed-in shopping thing in the old warehouse off the river, right?"

"Yes, there's a great bar in there that I think you'll like. But remember, I have a price. What can you tell me about you?" He smiled at her with warmth.

"There's nothing to tell you, but there's a lot you could tell me to help others."

"Wheels within wheels. I can tell you about Russian hacking, but frankly, they're pretty obvious about it. My family gets tips that are easy enough to purchase. For the right price and connections, the Russians are happy to share gossip said in front of smart devices. None of it's news."

"That's what you've got for me?"

"I know it's disappointing… like *your* answer." He took another sip, then moved his fingers to toy with the hem of her corset.

"What do you want to know?" Misha sighed. He was going to be disappointed with how little there was to know about her.

"You like to talk about families. Your mom seems to know a lot of people?"

"You want to know about my mom? She's a surgeon." Misha felt more relaxed again, but the conversation was all non sequiturs. It was hard to determine where this was all going.

"Misha, your mom is a *world-renowned* surgeon, and you happen to be a professor who starred in a sex scandal to become a researcher placed at an embassy. Your cover is your actual life. Who does that?" His hand tired of the hem and started to explore the terrain underneath.

"Are we playing Spy vs. Spy? What do you want?" She really should have left already, but something about the confusion intrigued her.

"Right now, I'm blowing your cover and trying to find out what's underneath it and under this. What do you think of my advanced interrogation techniques?" He began to kiss her neck and caress her hair as his other hand worked very slowly up the inside of her thigh.

"Excuse me if I don't want to talk about my family at this particular moment. Why don't you tell me something useful and see if it inspires me?" Misha took his hand away, climbed on top of him, and pressed her body against his.

In response, he leaned forward, his lips on her ear, and

whispered, "You're in real trouble. We can play around as much as you like, but you have to help me so I can keep you alive. I want to help you."

Misha pushed back and looked at him with surprise. But he continued to move, as if this was part of the seduction, although his expression had hardened. She stayed motionless.

"What do you say I grab one of the shitty reds, and we retire to bed for the night?" Mr. X's voice purred as his face kept the same rigid mask that showed Misha how serious he was.

"I'm sorry. I'm not feeling so well. How about we meet up tomorrow at the whale place?" She slowly unstraddled him and stood up. She went back to the kitchen to get covered up and collect her things. But he followed her, pulled out a bottle of red and began to open it.

"I'm serious. I'm leaving now. I'll see you tomorrow at ten."

"I know," he said, laughing. "This is for me. We'll talk more tomorrow."

"Sure." Misha put on the trench coat Jeff had given her and rushed back to her apartment by a new route.

CHAPTER 7

ABOVE GROUND, SUMMER WAS IN full swing. Senators had fled the hot, tourist-laden city for their respective districts or vacations with lobbyists of every ilk. Washington, D.C. reminded all that walked its streets that it was happiest as a swamp. Mosquitos and full humidity attacked the hair and skin of many an innocent bystander.

The break from serious matters for those above ground didn't apply to those below ground. The four people who'd previously occupied Boardroom M were there again, folders before them.

"The Thompson Report," the woman read.

"Isn't this the same one we approved last time, Carol?" the man in military attire asked testily.

"Is it?" Carol arched an eyebrow and glared at the two men across from her—the one with glasses and the one without.

"Umm, I'm not sure, General," said the one without glasses. "Yes… it might be."

"Fine," said the general gruffly. "What are the assets involved?"

"At this point, we can say that every branch of the highest levels of government is involved. Furthermore, there are now many non-governmental and non-military agencies involved and at least two other countries. Since we last discussed this problem, it's grown considerably in scope. The people I work with believe if we do a controlled burn of Thompson, we might staunch the wound and—"

"Philip, you're always so quick to burn. You need to calm down. Joshua?" Carol redirected the conversation.

"Well…" Joshua started slowly, keeping his eyes on Carol's hawkish gaze that had settled on Philip like he were a mouse. "There are the risks, as discussed during our last meeting. Boardrooms A and L have included some ideas on how to extricate ourselves from this unfortunate situation."

"We believe it's a go," Carol said flatly, without waiting for the general to say his line.

"Carol, it seems like several parties have voiced concerns," the general said.

"It's a bit unorthodox, but I believe the following Whale Addendum should sort out both issues to everyone's satisfaction." Carol smiled without cheer at the general. Philip and Joshua looked down at their folders like scolded school children and said nothing further.

"Very well, but let's keep it moving," the general added.

All four players flipped to the following page.

"The Whale Addendum," Carol read.

"What are the assets involved?" asked the man in military attire as he silently counted down the sheets until he could leave this farce of a meeting.

Joshua answered, "This can happen with a limited number of assets in Hungary: one minor U.S. diplomat who works for us. We'll also require a few agents from NBSZ and KNBSZ to complete this mission. It will be a relatively small operation."

"We believe it's a go," Carol added, without waiting for the question. "This should settle both situations with the least cost."

This time no-one objected, and they flipped over their sheets in unison.

CHAPTER 8

THE NIGHT HAD LOST ALL trace of sunset. Standing in the open-air atrium of the Hungarian ruin bar, Misha took in the visual spectacle. Art, color, and decrepitude surrounded her, closing in now the light of day had gone. The drug-induced sculptures seemed to move with the shifting of fairy lights and thumping music.

Misha's eyes traveled up the elaborate art deco walls rising four stories above her, imagining that this was what it would feel like to stand in the middle of a giant Bundt cake tin. She admired all the cracks in the faded veneer overhead. The cornices that were once intricately shaped and crafted gave way to inevitable decay of rot and mold. All the old-world beauty had slipped into a gothic Mad Max meets amusement park explosion. Despite all this, Misha enjoyed the view, as well as the goosebumps covering her skin. The cold air filled her lungs. She breathed deeply, feeling her little black dress tug against her chest.

There were few things as good as cold air for a night of excessive drinking. The people around Misha were full of joyful energy, fueled by a night of alcohol and drugs. They flitted up and down the stairs through thick brick archways and danced with abandon in every corner of the club.

Is all this rushing about really necessary? Misha wanted to yell. *Take your time! Enjoy the moment while you still can!* But she knew there was no point. Time came and went—no-one could live every second to the fullest. The reason for these feelings was the adrenaline that was starting to build up its acrid taste in the back of her throat. The danger was almost here. She lit a cigarette and slipped into memories of the last few weeks, memories that came to her in the dark, unbidden.

The meeting with Mr. X had been perfect in its precision. The meeting at the embassy gate where Misha couldn't quite find her badge was adorable. He fell for it so quickly. The tension between them grew so fast. During the day, she'd text Immie anything she could think of to make her smile. More and more, Immie would reply, but then the night would come, and Misha would give herself over to the mission and Mr. X. With him, things were easy, vague, and dangerous. He was her job, but he also offered refuge from her lack of physical connection in Hungary.

The rewards were substantial with this American playboy/diplomat. Until that night a couple of weeks ago when he changed the rules. He added complexity, and then he started ghosting her. That was when Misha felt the slow, tedious work pace of the regular CIA agent. She moved carefully and started to watch everything and everyone around her. She saw the world of the embassy and her role within its sphere.

Misha kept long hours at the embassy so that she could track Mr. X's comings and goings. Every day, he arrived between eleven and a quarter to noon, would leave for lunch at noon, and maybe return from three to five. He made an appearance like he was a Kardashian of public service. From what Misha could figure out now that she was watching Mr. X from outside of their relationship, he was placed here based on his lineage, complete with Olympic-level drinking abilities. He was uncomplicated, so

Misha knew he was exaggerating the dangers to her. He didn't talk to anyone, but he drank with everyone. There was no way this fool's warning the night in his apartment or the next day at the Bálna could be accurate. So she happily kept her distance from him while she tightened up her craft. He reciprocated by refusing to see her socially anymore. They were at a stalemate, or their love affair had burnt out. Maybe both.

Unfortunately, before things soured over coffee, Mr. X had given Misha one piece of information to pass onto the CIA. Misha filed it without mentioning that their "friendship" had ended. So the CIA kept her in place and pushed for more. Now Misha was stuck doing the tiresome task of actually spying. She failed to report the change in their status because she was sure that she would win in the end. The sex was fantastic: he couldn't possibly walk away from that? After four long, quiet workdays waiting for him to come back to her, she began to think she'd read the situation wrong.

Tired of waiting, Misha left a wireless earbud on his desk behind the computer and listened in to the comings and goings in his office. The first day, she listened as she scrolled through old photos. Mr. X took a call from a guy he called Benjamin. They met at a bar that night. The next day, she put her phone browser into private mode and watched porn for hours. Part of being an agent is acting like an average person. And humans who are rich and connected enough to get a research post in an embassy are as predictable in their shortcomings as everyone else: looking at vanilla porn on the phone at work was the most logical and strategic move. Meanwhile, Mr. X came in late, took no calls, and left for the day at one p.m. After a week that started out titillating and ended with her bored of watching people fly their freak flags, she began to get concerned. How much longer could she put off the office and cope with just sitting with nothing to do? Then there was the text message from Immie: "When are you coming home?"

Misha had to wrap this up and leave. Immie was way more important than some rich boy who was fucking with her time and not providing actual fucking anymore. And as if on cue, Misha heard clear as day in her ear, "Drinks tonight at the bar with the statue made of wood. Come and get your ear pod thing. This is pathetic." The timing couldn't have been better. Aside from Mr. X being right—the earbud move was a bit lowbrow—she couldn't be more pleased. Finally, she could fix things up with him enough to file the last report and get the hell out of this place.

She arrived at the bar around six. And waited. Mr. X seemed to enjoy making her wait, which she saw as a power move in retaliation for refusing to tell him any more about her life. But it didn't bother her. It wasn't like he was ever on-time for anything. The longer she waited for him, the more she combed her life for stories that seemed safe to share. She figured he wanted her to suffer a little and to spill when he arrived. Two could play that game, but she prepared to play it better. In the end, she decided to tell him about a time she nearly fell off her horse at summer camp. It was embarrassing, and she'd share with him the mostly true version, leaving out how she was attempting to shoot an apple off a fence while racing her horse downhill. Explaining how a nine-year-old was unsupervised with a horse and a handgun was harder to justify.

Hours passed. Misha finally concluded that Mr. X had stood her up. She'd have one more drink. When that was done, she'd quit waiting and go home. That was almost better than getting or giving intel. It was a believable half-truth: he'd opted out of being an asset. That sort of thing happens all the time. He'd already told her that he hated his family but loved their money. Misha had begun to relax, thinking through how she'd present this in her message to Jeff.

After finishing her drink, she realized that she didn't really want to go home yet. The intoxication and cool air felt good. In her reverie, she hadn't noticed the man in the black tailored t-shirt, gray blazer, and black cap-toed leather Oxfords standing in front of her. Getting lost in thought was not a good look. She needed to regain her focus. She pulled out a cigarette and lighter that had found their way into her purse. Sometimes, one needed a life-affirming activity when the day-to-day felt as dull as death.

"You can't smoke in here," the man said. He appeared to be studying her, not necessarily checking her out, but taking her all in.

"Who are you to say?" Misha replied in as haughty a tone as she could muster. A little defiance separated the nosey from the determined. It had got her out of a good deal of trouble over the years.

He took a step toward her. "Someone who's trying to keep you from getting kicked out." A thick Hungarian accent but perfect American phrasing.

"And why should you care if I do?"

His manner of speaking required more exploration. She had to keep him talking and see if she could get some idea of who he was, as far as threats and opportunities were concerned.

"If you leave now, I won't get to see you standing in the night air in that dress anymore. And I'll lose my chance to talk with you." His eyes twinkled with playfulness, but apart from this, nothing about his demeanor suggested that he was genuinely interested in seeing her stand here or anywhere.

Misha stared at him. Physically, he was unremarkable: average height, pleasant face, no noticeable marks or tattoos. Maintaining eye contact, Misha dropped her cigarette and crushed it with her toe. Something about this movement seemed to affect the man, but she ignored it and put on her best friendly American attitude, extending her hand and saying, "Thank you, um…?"

"Gellert." He raised his eyes as far as Misha's hand and shook it. His hand was warm, dry, and firm. "Have you been here long?" He didn't appear to be at all nervous. Misha wasn't sure this was good news or bad news.

"An hour," she lied. This guy wasn't giving away much, but Misha felt sure it was time to sober up because he seemed like trouble. His face, body, and words were all telling her different stories. She could kick herself for all of the drinking she'd done.

"So, your date has left, or did he not show?" He looked perturbed, as if a fly were circling around his head.

"Oh, you're sizing me up, I see. I've been stood up. I hope you don't judge me too harshly for my inability to get a man to show up for a drink." Misha laughed too loudly, hoping it would make her seem drunker than she was. Her best move for the moment was to get Gellert to vastly underestimate her while she willed her body to process the alcohol in her blood faster.

"No, I judge the man poorly for skipping out on a woman like you. Usually, though, American women come with a man—husband or boyfriend or something…"

Misha felt more confident that he'd judged her to be an easy mark and that he could be more direct in his approach. But the way he was looking at her, she wasn't entirely sure that he was interested in her sexually. It was still hard to read him: maybe he was drunk and struggling to keep his focus, or perhaps his attention was split? The former seemed likely in a bar, but the latter felt more plausible. Why did he want her attention? She was also beginning to wonder if Mr. X might, in fact, be somewhere close by.

"Well, there is indeed a man, but I'm not sure what happened.

It isn't like him. He's usually on time—at least he has been for the time I've known him. We work together, and I... well, I guess I read him wrong. It's a shame really. We were becoming such good friends. But that's how it goes sometimes." Misha shrugged and watched for his reaction. His face showed no recognition or concern, so she felt more confident that he didn't know Mr. X personally. The sour, battery taste returned to her throat. Her mind and body were concluding together that Gellert was a threat of some kind. Something was wrong.

"I need to get a glass of water. I'm afraid I've had too much to drink while I was waiting. I'll be right ba—"

"I'll get it for you." Gellert took off in the direction of the bar.

Misha's mind now had red sirens blaring, *Never let a stranger get you a drink*. But Gellert was gone, and there was no way for her to catch up to him without getting unwanted attention. Misha's body forced the tingly-brain feeling back and down as it went on full alert. She used the heightened energy to shape her focus.

Rapidly, she began to sort out how to make this new turn of events fit into her mission. An American-educated Hungarian trying to distract her wasn't how things were supposed to go, and it was an added layer of complexity. But it didn't mean she couldn't make this work: a mission is a mission is a mission.

Gellert returned.

"Misha, here's your water. Why don't we go and sit a moment while you drink it?"

Gellert knew her name. *Why would anyone in Hungary know or be interested in my whereabouts? This is a small operation, and it's as sanctioned as far as these things go. Intriguing. Time to push forward into the unknown.* "That sounds good."

As he led her through one of the arched doorways, Misha spilled half her drink on the ground. He continued up the stairs, looking over his shoulder twice to confirm that she was following.

Leaning into her cover, Misha performed an exaggerated stumble to spill more of her drink and hopefully convey that she was very tipsy. She reached into her memories for a clue as to what this could be all about, but she came up short. Mr. X not showing up made sense to her, but a man not trying very hard to hide that he was targeting her didn't. Or rather, it added up to be a real problem.

Mr. X didn't like that she was unwilling to tell him much about herself personally. It made him mad enough that he ended communication with her, but when did it become this, whatever "this" was?

Misha moved to take a seat with Gellert as she scanned the area of the second-floor bar with a view into the courtyard. There were very few people around in this section of the bar. Placing her elbow on the table and her chin in her hand, she stared at the midground and said, "What's your name again?"

"Ah, yes.…" Gellert paused and looked in the direction of the balcony. "Gellert. We met by the tree when you were smoking."

"Right. Right. Gellert, what do you do?"

"I manage this establishment."

"So, you were saving yourself from having to kick me out?" Misha sprawled out in the chair and took the smallest sip from her glass, which wasn't hard, as she'd spilled the majority walking up the stairs. She wanted to give the impression that she'd drunk most of it and was starting to feel sleepy. Misha wasn't sure, but given the situation, it seemed likely the water had been drugged. It was a risky presumption, but if worse came to worse, she could play it off as the intoxication from drinking, which was leaving her tired anyway.

"Exactly. You've done me a great honor in helping you stay. What is it that you do, Misha?"

"Professional failure turned dating fiasco." Misha shrugged.

She dreaded the direction of this, but like any coming disaster, she couldn't stop herself from rushing to the conclusion. "My head is spinning. I think I need to call it a night. Maybe I'll come visit you another time."

"I have an office that's much quieter if you need a moment to recover. It's too soon to leave."

"I'm afraid I won't be much of a conversationalist. I better be getting home."

"If you wish." Gellert, would-be destroyer of spies, had no sparkle in his eyes: they were flat and dull. There seemed to be a thick curtain between his inner and outer world. He stood and offered Misha his hand.

Misha was on full alert now. Her playing tired seemed to fit into his scheme. She appreciated his short answers, allowing her time to scan the room and strategize about her options. As she noted the place, the exits, and the people, she prepared for a complicated extrication. Giving her hand to this Gellert, she made a big show of having difficulty standing. He reached a warm arm around her waist and half-carried her the first couple of steps. Then, like a drunk, she pushed him away to create some physical space. She noted how he was leading her back into the building instead of downstairs toward the street. Her fear seemed confirmed by this action: the water had been drugged.

Misha followed him through a few rooms and then faked a slip to grab his pants. She could feel something hard near his belt and understood that this man was likely going to try and kill her. Misha was attempting to come up with a good solution, but was thwarted by her drink-dulled thinking. Eventually, they ended up in the hallway of an abandoned wing of the building, a part that looked like it was reliving the bombings from a bygone era.

Gellert took a comically large key from his pocket and unlocked a door. Misha quickly reviewed the turns and distance from her spot at the tree to this location. She was unlikely to have time to contemplate whether it was a right-right-left or a left-left-right on her run out. As Gellert opened the door, Misha's first view was of a table in the middle of a room that had walls of crumbling plaster. Exposed beams on the ceiling looked like they mightn't be able to hold the walls from collapsing. The table was delicate and well preserved in comparison to its surroundings. Misha walked slowly to the table and then leaned heavily against it, making a show of needing it for support. Gellert closed the door, locked it, and pocketed the key.

Misha took a deep breath as she prepared herself. This moment was where all of her training was going to save her life. She was not a maiden in distress but an agent who'd trained for moments like this. At her twelve o'clock was a filing cabinet. At two o'clock was a mop and a bucket. Her six was Gellert and the door. And at her nine were two old chairs with a table between them. Apart from this, the room was more or less barren.

Gellert grabbed her hair and shoved her, face down, onto the table, pressing his forearm into her spine. Time for planning was over, but it made Misha's opening move more apparent. "Why the rush? No foreplay?"

Gellert stepped back a foot, laughing, but not in a happy way. "Don't move."

"No," Misha whispered as she slid down into a squat and spun to the side. This action was not what Gellert was expecting as he came down with his arm again, pinning nothing but the air to the table. Misha punched him in the crotch with her elbow to give herself room to get the table between them. Then she grabbed the mop and broke it over her knee, thankful for a weapon.

Gellert responded by placing the key on the table. "We've had a misunderstanding. I thought you wanted to be alone with me," he said, although his eyes and body remained silent on the subject.

"You think a woman likes to be bent over a table and pinned down?" Misha played the wide-eyed ingénue, surprised by his lack of understanding about intimacy. Tentatively, she reached for the key. He came down fast to grab her wrist, and she leveraged the broken mop against the table more quickly. Gellert impaled himself. She let out a sigh of relief. He wasn't dead, but he'd fallen for the move, which meant he believed that she was significantly impaired and not able to defend herself. Misha pressed against the back of his head with one hand, using his unstable angle to drive the broken mop handle further inside him. Then she got behind him, reached around the band of his pants, and there it was: a P9RC. He'd so underestimated her that he never even tried for it.

Misha stood in Gellert's view to ask him why he was here. But he was gurgling, and his breath was getting more shallow. The eyes that looked through and beyond her were now growing cloudy and distant. His time for answering questions had passed. She squeezed his hand and talked to him in soothing tones until he stopped moving, stopped breathing. Killing someone was part of her job, but no-one could stop her from being a human.

Alone in the room with the neutralized threat, Misha turned her attention to sorting through the events. Mr. X had planned this meeting, Mr. X no-showed, and a man showed up to do what to her? They wanted her drugged, but most likely not dead, not immediately anyway. The dead Gellert carried a military handgun, so this was probably an intelligence operation. Why would Hungarians, or anyone in the region, want Misha? She had no specific information that would serve the Hungarians, Russians, or anyone else. She was on her first mission to get information about Russian ties to America, but she didn't have anything of value for anyone.

Then the cabinet caught her eye. It probably held club-related documents, but since she was here, it was worth checking. She kept the gun in one hand, in case another operative showed up. The lock on the cabinet was simple enough. She opened it in minutes. Just what she'd thought: mostly employment documents. One folder, though, looked curious, so she took out her phone to photograph it and saw she'd missed a call from Immie. She listened to the voicemail as she snapped the photos. She'd transmit them later. Immie was explaining that without waiting for Misha, she'd met with a real estate broker, who said they could get a reasonable price for their house. Misha would need to process that later, as this was the first time she'd heard anything about selling their house.

On the upside, this meant she was getting cell phone reception. So she called in support and texted her location. As she waited, she continued to go through files, but they just confirmed her first impression. Then she combed the room for any hidden boxes, information, or anything else of note. There was nothing. She moved on to checking Gellert, but as she'd also expected, there was no ID on him.

Misha swept the room twice before her backup arrived. She let her in and provided a quick debrief, with a warning that there might be other agents floating around somewhere. Her backup listened attentively and then said, "You've got eighteen minutes to clear a mile radius."

Misha ran out, scanning for possible interference. She continued down the stairs and out of the bar without seeing anything out of place. Running counter-surveillance tactics to lose likely tails and to evade detection, she walked the night streets of Budapest, in and out of bars, doubling back down lanes, and finally along the Danube. When it appeared in all ways clear, she transmitted her photos in two bursts, disassembled the key phone components, and threw the pieces into the river below.

Walking from the river, Misha nearly missed it—a move from the right in the shadows. She jumped back as a motorcycle flew past her and onto the road. She continued walking toward her apartment. Then she heard it before she saw it—the bike had circled, and the rider had taken a shot at her. She ran forward in the direction of her apartment and took cover in the next alley. Another agent was waiting for her. He slammed her hard against the brick wall, but she stayed conscious. She responded to his attack with a full-body lunge, but his lithe shape clearly hid that he must be all muscle because he barely moved. He took a step back to throw a punch, but Misha blocked it. They fought more, with the agent taking a few blows to the face and kidneys, and Misha to the head and chest. Then he got Misha's back against the wall. He went to punch her face, but she moved quickly, and he broke his hand on the wall.

Misha didn't think she'd get lucky a second time, so she pulled away, putting distance between them. That gave her the time and space to pull Gellert's gun out of her coat pocket. She wasn't supposed to keep it, let alone use it on the streets of Budapest, but it was necessary. She shot at the agent but missed his chest, winging him in the shoulder. There was still enough distance. She aimed and got the head shot.

The shots would attract a lot of unwanted attention, including from the man on the motorcycle. She looked around the corner and saw an empty street with parked cars. The bike and rider could be anywhere, but she couldn't see them. There were lights on in a few windows. Misha calculated and picked an alley up ahead that she could follow to her secondary route home. Ducking down and gathering all her strength, she ran serpentine and low. There was nothing. No sound.

Misha continued to scan, plan, and move. With each block, she thought she might be getting away from her assailant but didn't really believe it would be that easy. She figured it would be best to work around toward her apartment and away from her primary extraction point. Luckily, they were within a few blocks of each other.

Misha made it to her one-bedroom without running into anyone. She knew these buildings well, and this knowledge afforded her some advantage. With the door locked, she slid into protocols and procedures. First, a quick email sent to "mother," to get out a warning and a request for help. Then she watched her security cameras. Everything looked quiet. She wanted to be busy to distract herself from the burning feeling in her stomach from operating on adrenaline for too long. There was an email from "mother" with the code for "We'll send a team to the secondary site," which was two blocks from her apartment. As she prepared to leave her building, Misha checked her security cameras one more time and saw the motorcyclist approaching her building from the south.

She grabbed her go bag, the gun, and her laptop and took off through the north exit route. She panted and promised her body it could relax in three blocks. Shadow to shadow and doorway to doorway, she picked her way across the three streets that felt like three miles until she was secure with her extraction team. Now she would have to get out of Hungary, get a new phone, and call Immie back to figure out why they were selling the house. Misha wondered if Immie would back down if she casually mentioned that she nearly died three times today.

CHAPTER 9

"DID YOU SEE THE NEWS this morning? Not good." Jeff was seated at a table, scrolling through his tablet.

"Please speak quietly. I'm feeling very fragile." Misha slunk onto the couch to drink her coffee. It had been a long night, jammed behind barrels in the back of a cold, dark freight truck, with only a bottle of cheap liquor for comfort. She wasn't sure if she was awake and hungover, or awake and drunk.

"Apparently, the body of an unidentified man has been found, with a chest wound."

"Oh, really. Where was that?" Misha tilted her head and looked blankly back at Jeff. "What's the world coming to when a man can't drug and isolate a woman in a crumbling back office without ending up with a three-inch hole through this rib cage?"

Not that Misha felt great about the experience. She'd thought about this when the adrenaline wore off as they drove into Austria. In the relative safety of this small modern apartment, it was difficult for Misha to stop imagining someone missing Gellert today. Maybe someone was having a smoke on a stoop, thinking of his friend or family member. She thought of how Immie might feel if Misha had been killed instead. She needed to believe that even if Immie didn't want her anymore, she'd at least regret her demise.

"Did you also see the article on how a local female law enforcement agent 'found' some documents that exposed an underground crime ring? It looks like Budapest is leading the way to a more civil society," Misha added.

Jeff's glare in response to her sarcasm suggested he wasn't in the mood for Misha's shenanigans. But they were both breathing and in the same place, so there'd be shenanigans regardless of his mood.

They were both quiet for a while. Then some sounds coming from another part of the apartment grabbed Misha's full attention. She straightened her spine and tried to clear her head.

Into the room strolled Max, wearing his signature Hawaiian t-shirt.

Misha relaxed a bit. "Max?"

"Good morning, kiddos." The older man smiled warmly, as if he'd just bumped into them at a local bar. He joined Jeff at the table but positioned himself so he could look both of them in the eye and also watch what was happening outside the window.

"I didn't know you were here," Misha said, eyeing him with suspicion.

"And hopefully no-one else knows either. The three of us need to talk through some things. It turns out that there's been some… difficulty… with you joining the company. I didn't think it would go like this." His eyes sparkled as if he anticipated something exciting happening, but then his voice trailed off like he wasn't sure what to say next.

Jeff put down his tablet and gave his undivided attention to Max, a thing Misha had never seen him do for anyone before.

"Misha. Jeffery. There are some things that we need to discuss now before anything else happens. Jeff, I suppose you've already told Misha that you've been her handler for many years now?" Seeing both Jeff and Misha's surprise at this, Max added quickly, "It wasn't far out of his way, Misha. You're the friend he's always needed."

Misha looked over to see Jeff sheepishly studying his hands.

"You came to UNC to meet me?" Misha wasn't sure she was following what Max was trying to say.

"Misha, I made sure you got the professorship." Jeff's face softened with the memory of those years. "It was the best my job has ever been. You're a delight, and I love you, but yes, you're also my job and responsibility. I'm in charge of your safety. I… we… thought it was time to put you in a position where I could do that officially." Jeff froze and looked to Max for help. How much was he supposed to say?

"What Jeff doesn't know and what we need to discuss now is why I needed him to recruit you at a glacial pace. You have to realize that most agents are recruited in months and then trained over a year or years. They aren't best friends with a handler and then randomly swept up as agents, as in your case. You should have died last night: you don't have official training for the level of agents you were up against. Last night, you proved that the project works." Max looked at her with what appeared to be pride.

Misha attempted to process Jeff's and Max's words, but whether due to the drinking or the shock of the night before, it all sounded like garbage. She wanted to talk to Immie, to have a relatively normal conversation with someone, but she'd need a new phone for that.

Max continued, "Imagine for a second that nothing in your life happened by accident. That when you got up in the morning, a team of people were figuring out how to encourage you to be stronger and to do better. As the years passed, the team would grow, and they'd work to give you opportunities to develop and advance in your areas of strength." He paused. He'd dreamt of this conversation for years, had practiced it so many times and in so many ways, but it was coming out all wrong.

Misha looked between the two men, trying to understand what was going on. What was Max saying? Jeff had taken her to UNC and got her first job as a professor? That was part of grooming her to become an agent a decade later? It didn't make any sense. She was definitely still drunk.

"Let me try this another way," Max said. "I was a successful agent and bureaucrat in the '70s. We were in Vietnam, and the Cold War was hot. Twelve of us, with different areas of expertise, were put in a room together and told to come up with a solution to end the Cold War. We sat together in this secret meeting— day in and day out—for weeks. We discussed philosophy, war, diplomacy, and anything else we thought could lead to a stronger America and, ultimately, to a better world." He paused to ensure he had their attention, as if he were teaching a course on global politics to distracted freshmen.

"Well, in the end, the room was split. We had twelve different solutions that each of us was certain was the correct one, but these solutions could be divided into two distinct camps. One believed the only way to succeed, especially with a foe as strong as the Russians, was to fight every battle with better equipment and such force that we'd inspire fear in all who attempted to stand against us. I'll call this group the Gears, because they continue like clockwork until things stop dead. And you can see the handiwork of the Gears in all levels of our government: Iran–Contra, coups, assassinations that everyone suspects our country orchestrated, and billions of dollars a year that go into defense. Do you follow so far?"

"Yes, our country is the top spender on the military in the world. Some people say that this makes the world less safe, not to mention putting a target on our country, citizens, and service members." Misha looked back at him, feeling like this conversation could have been covered by watching Fareed Zakaria for an hour. But like a consummate college student, she could be drunk and participate in any lecture.

"Right. I was in the other camp. Those five other members and I had grown up with the stories of the great deeds done by men and women during World War II. They were our parents and teachers. We saw what the Gears of the Third Reich had attempted to do to humanity, and we found ourselves drawn to the intelligent, dangerous work done by the OSS in the U.S. and the SIS in the UK. Our group was curious about using strategy and kindness to win territory, if you will. Our philosophy included the way Israelis use psychology to screen passengers at airports and how the British gave German officers lovely houses and anything they asked for, while secretly recording their conversations to get quality intel. I'll call *our* group the Water because we too believed in winning against our enemies slowly by seeming to flow with and around them.

"Since the two camps were divided, in the end, someone needed to make a call. The president was called upon to cast the deciding vote. He opted for a compromise: we'd follow a combination of the ideas of both the Gears and the Water. War is often a short and fast game, so we continued the Gear policy on the surface. Watch the news any day of the week, and this is no surprise. However, the Water plan takes time to build, so we were provided with the resources and opportunities to create a situation to take tasks on as we were ready."

Again Max paused, reviewing everything he'd just said to make sure he didn't leave anything out. He continued, "I was part of a few projects for the Water, most of which came to nothing, but a few of them are still in place today, with varying degrees of success. There was one project that I took on alone to create the best agents I possibly could. I planned to use everything we knew about education, spies, and getting information out of people and then raise children with those skills. Don't worry. It wasn't like I was grabbing children and putting them in specialist spy schools—the Communists were doing that successfully, and they still do. Instead, I worked with the children's parents, many of whom were agents themselves, and we looked for opportunities for the kids to grow in this way. The project was extremely costly because the kids lived all over the country, and it takes a lot of money to get resources slipped in without it being noticed.

"Time passed, and eventually, my project was forgotten in the halls of Washington. I still had resources and money, but it was made clear to me that no-one wanted a progress report or to see any of my agents go into the field. All of my child spies remain blissfully unaware of how talented they are or the extent of their capacities. There's this one sleeper who could give Seal Team 6 a run for their money, and he's a dentist." Max chuckled. "Can you believe it: all that talent, and he does perfect dentistry?"

"And?" Misha felt like she was in a Disney movie and would now find out she's from a distant planet or has superhuman strength. Maybe this was some hazing for blowing her first assignment.

"And," Max replied delicately, "I was happy for my kids to be excellent without ever lifting a finger for their government because they served our society so well every day. My superhumans are exceptional in their careers, they serve their communities, and they're good people. These actions are also a gift to our country. But one of my sleepers was exposed, and it appears that she's now a known quantity to the group of twelve. And I don't believe she's safe anymore, despite my best efforts." He stopped again and looked at Misha expectantly.

"Me? My head's throbbing. Can we stop with this?" Misha went to the kitchen to get some water but ended up vomiting into the sink instead. Max and Jeff waited while Misha composed herself, poured a glass of water, and rejoined them in the living room.

"Yes, Misha, you've always been a favorite of mine. Your mom is one of the best agents I've had the privilege of knowing."

"My mom's a surgeon."

"Yes, she's that too." The word *too* made Misha feel nauseated again.

"Misha, it's the truth," Jeff said. "I was supposed to get you the professorship. I even had a hand in a few other things in your life. When that book came out, we tried to write it off as a fluke. We didn't know it was going to take such a toll on you. In the end, we thought maybe if we put your training to use, you'd be happier. We hadn't planned for how ill-equipped you were to handle failure. Then you succeeded beyond our expectations at training, so we put you in the field, thinking this was your second act. But last night taught us two things: that book was intended to flush you out, and your training has been successful. There's no way a new agent would survive what you survived last night."

"You all had something to do with that book?" Anger was building in Misha's voice.

"No!" they both exclaimed.

Jeff looked at her with fear in his eyes. "That book's a farce, but we can't draw attention to it. We had to let you lose your job. The plan was to get you into the service and out of the public eye. But it was too late. Budapest showed us that. Budapest was a strategic attack, Mish. The man you killed—it shouldn't have been possible."

"That's why I'm here, Misha. The three of us need to come up with a plan. Your life depends on it. I don't know who wants you exposed or dead: this project was supposed to die with me, so there's no point in hurting any of the participants. You were all supposed to live blissfully unaware of your roles. Between the three of us, we should be able to figure this out." Max looked at Jeff and Misha with hope.

Misha sipped her water. It wasn't the right time to request a new cell phone. With her stomach empty and her head full of storm clouds, all she wanted was take a nap, but she forced herself to focus on interpreting what she'd heard. "So, my mother, *Doctor* Campbell, is a spy and an old friend of yours, Max? You both worked to create a spy out of me, but then spies fell out of fashion, so you thought there was no harm in me working as a professor. Then someone got an old boyfriend to write a book to destroy my career, accusing me of things I didn't do. And you decided to make me a spy anyway because that was safer somehow. But that turned out to be a dumb idea, and whoever wanted me exposed in the first place now wants me dead. And because of the now constant and clear danger to my life, you thought it might be a good idea to tell me that I'm a product of your top-secret spy training camp. Do I have the rough idea here?"

"There was no top-secret training camp: that was the whole point. Only one person knows about the spies in the program, and that's me," Max answered.

"Don't forget my mother, Jeff, and anyone else you brought onto your little team. It seems like the only people unaware are the spies themselves. You're also leaving out why anyone wants this program exposed." Misha was so angry that a part of her wanted to write it all off as impossible and be done with it.

"I have a theory," Max said. "It has two parts. One is that the Gears have made so many mistakes that people who know about these things are looking more into the Water programs. I think maybe my program is most up to speed, but I don't understand how anyone would have the name of any of the participants. The second part is that when the president made his decision, we created a way to meet and move the programs forward: we call it the Boardroom. I haven't gone to a meeting in ages, but they still take place. I must have been careless with something, and they figured out you were a part of it. I think they wanted to see if you were spy material. What I can't figure out is who on the board cares this much. If they really wanted the program gone, they should have come for me. I wonder if one of the Gears wants to use the spies to push forward their war agenda."

"You're right, Misha," Jeff said. "We got played, and we fell for it. Last night, I almost lost you, which would have been unacceptable, both professionally and personally. I've been cavalier because I didn't believe Max. I didn't think anyone was looking for you or testing you. Now there's no other explanation. We need to move forward with a plan, and there's no plan without including you from now on. And when we figure out who this person is, I'm going to destroy them."

"If you two are right, we should get out of this apartment now. They'll be looking for me." Misha didn't know what to do with the anger and confusion clouding her mind, so instead she leaned into her spy training.

"We're not at a sanctioned safehouse, but that's still a decent call." Jeff looked from Misha to Max. "We'll meet at the plane and continue this conversation there. You're going to be fine, Misha. We'll figure this out."

Max didn't say any more. He just stood up, nodded to Misha, and walked out. Jeff then left the room and returned with a small suitcase.

"You and I need to do some prep work before we can leave this apartment. What would you prefer being: a redhead or a blonde?"

CHAPTER 10

TOP SECRET

CENTRAL INTELLIGENCE AGENCY

COUNTRY:USA   REPORT NO:███████

SUBJECT:Ubiytsa   DATE:████████████

NO. PAGES:2

REFERENCES C4A678, █████, BB389S

DATE OF INFO:█████████████

PLACE & DATE ACQ.: Budapest, Hungary

This is UNEVALUATED Information

SOURCE: A reliable agent placed at the embassy

1. Throwaway, referred to as Ubiytsa, escaped and
    was not rolled up. Source observed Ubiytsa enter
    and leave the premises. Further, observed a
    female Hungarian police officer enter the loca-
    tion after Ubiytsa. Source voiced concerns that
    this officer is window dressing for counter-
    espionage efforts.

2. Source believes Ubiytsa killed the raven from NSBZ. All information on this raven is being sanitized. Another raven is in the wind.

3. Intel about Ubiytsa's ability was inaccurate. Ubiytsa is extremely dangerous, and further intel is required to resolve the issue.

4. The source is demanding more information, specifically whether Ubiytsa is a double or a mole.

5. Source has threatened to use his family's connections against agency if he is not moved immediately and all contact with Agent Carol is stopped.

TO: Central Intelligence Agency
Attention: ███████████

FROM: ██████
SUBJECT: Ubiytsa—Action Necessary

1. Forwarded as Attachment A, intelligence from a witness about Ubiytsa neutralizing what we know to be a senior NSBZ officer with advanced training. The loss of this agent has caused unexpected blowback and multiple sanitization issues.

2. Ubiytsa is currently en route to Tulsa for an observe and report. The agent will be occupied for five days. Prepare a plan at this time.

3. Recommend liquidation of Ubiytsa on foreign soil by a team of foreign agents with enhanced training. Protocol: Whiskey Bravo Golf Kilo

   a. Resolve the blowback with NSBZ. Though we will need to offer additional chicken feed to resolve fully.

   b. Liquidity will thaw the region.

   c. Gather more intel on Ubiytsa to complete the next mission to satisfaction.

CHAPTER 11

MISHA HAD NO CLUE HOW she found herself in Tulsa, Oklahoma, but here she was, watching a Nebraska–beef-fed collegiate walk into a barbershop after following him since he left the hotel he was staying in using Daddy's credit card. Who gets themselves sent to middle America, a place lacking in coastal views and liberal ideals? Sure, there might be a few liberal-leaning people who don't fit the mold of the church-going conservative, but for the most part, those who don't conform leave, one way or another. Misha hated the Midwest because her parents raised her among these good Christian folk who spoke a language she never learned. Now she stood on the sidewalk, contemplating how every decision her parents had made years ago was intentional and had led to her standing in a black trench coat on a corner in Tulsa, looking like something out of a Spy vs. Spy comic.

Although it had crossed Misha's mind that growing up in the Midwest was all part of "the plan," as Max called it, she dismissed this thought, along with almost everything else Max and Jeff had told her. Even if it was the truth, what good was that knowledge to her? She was walking around with a target on her back and working for an organization that was very good at hitting targets.

Twenty minutes later, the collegiate emerged with a haircut that wasn't much different than the one he had when he entered. Misha followed him from a reasonable distance and watched him enter a coffee shop. For the next five days, this young man was Misha's job: a watch and report. Fresh from her brush with death in Hungary and straight into the flyover region of the United States to watch a child. At least this child had decided to blow off Shamrock, Texas, for the more urban climes of Tulsa, four hours away.

From the coffeehouse to a mom-and-pop auto shop. Misha smiled, imagining Kevin Bacon jumping out of nowhere to teach this youth how to dance in this religious town. She waited for the boy to step inside the shop so she could slip the tracker into the wheel well of the Dodge Ram he'd dropped off this morning. Tradecraft had taught her to stop somewhere close and make sure all the tech was working appropriately, while watching and waiting, and then watch and wait some more. But this was too depressing, so she headed straight to a hotel bar downtown.

Lots of Misha's friends in Berkeley, when she had friends and a life in Berkeley, felt strongly about local dive bars—the whole "support local" thing and the beauty of old fading wood and upholstery. But not Misha, who thought the whole hipster love of the past was yet another fake, classist thing. Like they know what it means to be poor because they once bought a Miller High Life during happy hour for a local tradesman, while they were getting fucked up on top-shelf liquor. Misha never wanted to feel a connection with her drinking buddies or the venue. She leaned toward the sanitized, corporate boringness of hotel bars, with people who were likely to just be passing through. The crisp martini in a suit talking with a co-worker, or a high-priced prostitute who charged for discretion. Misha liked these places because the drinks were good and there was privacy if you wanted it.

Misha sat down at a smooth, generic bar and ordered an Old Fashioned with a smoked bourbon. It was crafted by a millennial bartender whose ironically styled facial hair showed that he considered slinging cocktails to be an art. It also showed that he was going to fuck it up and take too long in doing so. This gave Misha time to think through how she could accomplish this ridiculous mission by doing the smallest amount of work possible. The rest of her time could be spent on something useful, like writing rambling love texts to Immie and masturbating.

The mission was simple: track the movements of one Trevor Hill, while he was home from A&M. And since he decided to blow off home for Tulsa, Misha was afforded more creature comforts. She'd already determined that he was a gentleman for this choice alone.

There were no hints, no context, no other communications to outline what Misha was supposed to look for while she was on this mission. Basic background research revealed that Trevor Hill was a sophomore at A&M, with unremarkable grades. He came from a family that had a reasonable nest egg from the reserves of oil under their equally unremarkable ranch. From initial observation, Trevor was boring in every way imaginable. He didn't drink, do drugs, fuck, chase, kill, or swear. He did seem to be busy though, doing little errands and chores, presumably for his dad or in preparation for the upcoming semester. Misha found herself wondering for the umpteenth time if it was possible to file a report that said, "I don't give a fuck about this kid, and you shouldn't either."

"Hey, bartender, can I have a cocktail napkin?"

The bartender nodded, but it was hard to tell if it was in answer to Misha's request or in accompaniment to the music playing in his head.

Misha added under her breath, "And my fucking drink."

A minute later, the bartender brought both, then stood there without saying a word. Misha took a sip of the cocktail and was surprised to say with full sincerity that it was delicious. He responded with the same general nod and what might have been a smile under the mass of hair on his upper lip and then walked away. Misha wasn't sure if they were communicating with each other, but she found herself warming to him and his facial hair with each sip.

Misha took a pen out of her trench coat inner pocket and picked up the napkin. It would be good to think through the things that had happened to her recently. Maybe they were just the normal twists and turns of the job of a spy? But she doubted that any other spies had been told that they'd been groomed for the role their entire life and were part of a conspiracy. She began writing on the napkin:

1. Jeff is a spymaster.

2. *That reads sexier than it is. I mean, Jeff is hot and all, but the idea that he's also a sexy spy and chosen to be my best friend? That's a very generous training program.*

3. Things with Immie are ending.

4. *Is that true? We met over the weekend to discuss the house and our relationship. Then we talked about how much I need to travel for the new job and how she wants me to find a different position. How does one say, "I can't simply quit working for the U.S. government under clandestine services," without saying "U.S." or "clandestine"? So the conversation degenerated and ended with Immie throwing a glass against the wall and screaming, "I fucking hate you!" I'm going to go with my wife hates me, and this isn't going to work out.*

5. Random hire tried to kill me in a Budapest bar and somehow also provided me with convenient access to useful documents.

6. *That one was especially weird. I spent a week thinking I was Kurt Russell in that What do you Give a Millionaire for his Birthday?—a terrifying "choose your own adventure." There hasn't been a party, but let's not rule that out yet. What was that movie called? Wait, that wasn't Kurt Russell. It was Michael Douglas. The Birthday? The Game? The Birthday Game?*

7. I know nothing.

8. *Accurate. This is so accurate I should probably change my name to Jon Snow from* Game of Thrones.

9. I trust no-one.

10. *Not entirely true. I trust that Jeff will always be the version of Jeff I know, even if that isn't who he is. But I'm in no rush to meet the "real" Jeff, in case I've been getting the Disney version all these years. I trust Immie, but she doesn't seem inclined to stay in my life. Though trusting either of these people is unlikely to be helpful.*

11. I'm still pissed about losing my job.

12. *Do I believe that the book is part of a… a what?*

13. I like making lists.

All true, and all probably better left unwritten. What does this tell me? I'm not living my best life, and maybe I should read something from the Oprah booklist? I doubt even Oprah could help me now. And who is this asshole who just sat next to me in an empty bar?

Misha turned her head slightly to see that her new elbow buddy was not some horny businessperson looking for a one-night stand. It was the boy she was supposed to be following without him knowing.

"Good evening, Trevor. Are you old enough to sit here?"

"Good evening, Misha." He nodded toward the napkin without giving her time to respond. "I can help you with your problem before you waste any more perfectly good napkins. Lougheed and Rekhter invented the Border Gateway Protocol using two napkins. Anything less than BGP is a waste of a napkin."

"I have no clue what you just said, but I'm pretty sure it was an insult." Misha studied Trevor's face, trying to work out his intent.

"No BGP, no internet. Your napkin doesn't replace the current techniques involved in making the internet work. Hence, it's a waste of a napkin."

"You're far more interesting to listen to than to follow. Do you know that?" Misha returned to her drink. Nothing about his face or body language posed a threat.

"You don't even know the half of it. Why don't you buy a guy a drink and see what he knows?"

"What would you like?"

"I don't know. I'm only seventeen. Are martinis good?"

"You're not seventeen." For a second, she was unsure if she was right about his age. This kid talked fast and didn't seem to stick to one lane. This conversation might require her to be both sober and drunk simultaneously.

"No, I'm twenty-three, and I made my first fake ID when I was sixteen. I've been drinking for a minute, but it's fun to push you off your mark for a second." He smirked. "Make it dirty, and don't use the well. I don't want a headache tomorrow."

"Barkeep, an extra dirty gin martini for my salty friend,

please. Aviation or the Botanist if you've got it. If you don't, make it Hendrick's."

The bartender smiled. *Hey, I guess we are communicating, even if just through pretentious drink orders.*

"You sure don't seem concerned that I'm sitting here and talking to you," Trevor said, looking mildly surprised.

"What if I told you I was talking it over with the napkin, and we were five minutes away from saying fuck this and heading out of town? You sitting here means that for a couple more minutes at least, I'm not a quitter. So, let's sit and chat. I think it may be the most entertaining part of my day." Misha was surprised that she jumped to sincerity in the conversation. Her training told her to lie and leave immediately, but her intuition told her this was going somewhere, and blunt conversation was the tool.

"Woah, you are deep in the weeds. Okay, barkeep, a second for my aged and jaded friend." Trevor smirked. "I feel sorry for you, and I'm going to help you out, but I'm not going to do the work for you. Make it interesting for me and ask me a question." It was a simple request, yet the look on his face was like a child at Christmas. He seemed eager to be asked a question.

"I think I was on this date fifteen years ago. Are you always so cocky?"

He is cocky, and I really ought to be guarded, but talking to him makes me feel like I'm with my younger brother (if I had one). I want to tousle his hair and tease him about the girls and guys at his school.

"Okay. Why are you in this bar? Are you following me?" Misha asked. *That seems like a safe enough question to ask an A&M sophomore on the government's naughty list.*

"Why are you following *me?*"

"Following orders. I'm here to watch you for a little less than a week, with no clarification. The rest is, as they say, classified."

"Yes, sorry about that, but I wanted you to work for it a

little bit." He then smiled like the cat that caught the canary. He grabbed a cherry from the garnish bucket and ate it.

Misha watched Trevor's poor manners and found them disgustingly charming. She suspected that he was unaccustomed to following rules. They were going to be friends. "You wanted me to work for what exactly?"

"I'm going to explain your napkin problem. I'm going to help you out a lot, but I want to reassure myself you're worth helping. So, ask me an *interesting* question. Don't be boring, or I'm going to jet, and you'll never see me again."

Misha felt her head swimming a bit, like she knew this young man, or she'd finally met her match. It was both an uncomfortable and an enjoyable experience. It felt right not to control the situation and to let someone else take the lead. She figured there was a better than sixty per cent chance that this kid wasn't going to try and kill her.

I'm sure Trevor's all bluster, and I don't know that he has anything to offer me. However, as I was going to quit anyway, and if there's the possibility of getting something I need, then I should at least try. Let's see—I asked him why he was following me, he wants me to work for the information, he's prepared to share…. What can I ask him about my "napkin problem" that would be illuminating? Hmm…

"Why does anyone want me as a spy?" *That feels like the obvious question in this situation, where my mark is following me, instead of vice versa.*

"You'd be better at asking questions if you think first. That's a hard question. First, this is going to surprise you, but you're well suited to your line of work, and for a newbie, you've gained a lot of attention. If it weren't for the second part, you'd be a rising star in clandestine services. For example, you're exceedingly good at getting people to share things and do things they wouldn't usually do. Second, they need *you*, specifically, to be a spy. And unfortunately, there's a split mind on why they need this. It turns out you know all the right 'wrong' people." Trevor said the last part with air quotes, which made Misha laugh.

But he didn't seem concerned by Misha's reaction and continued, "That's why I had to meet you. I wanted to know who this person was who found herself caught in the middle. It's like a multinational corporation is going through a shift, and there are two different departments needing to do research and development. Amazingly, you're the perfect scientist for both departments, and your choice will lead to one department rising, while the other will fall. I've been looking forward to meeting you. I'm a bit of a fanboy. You're like the Manchurian Candidate for two different parties at the same time."

"I don't understand. That was four different analogies crushed together. And more to the point, how do you *know* any of this shit you're saying?" Misha was slowly admitting to herself that the things Trevor was saying shared some striking similarities with what Max had told her a couple of weeks before. But it was no easier to listen to second time around.

"Okay, the questions are getting better now. Thank you. Right. I'm what you might call insatiably curious. I always have been, and I don't see me stopping anytime soon. So I read a lot. But I don't go to the library: my fascination is with the present, not the past. I like to know the non-watered down version of everything. So I've taken it upon myself to be a Wikileaks of one. I read through the internet to remind myself that politicians, companies, and governments are agencies run by real people with real shortcomings and not the Illuminati I heard about as a child.

"My father is a disabled vet. The decisions his superior officers made destroyed parts of him that are never coming back. It was too hard for him to believe that mere humans could commit the atrocities that lead to Gulf War Syndrome—he still believes in Mister Rogers' Neighborhood. There's no way he can believe average people could cause such harm. Hence, he thinks the Illuminati is running the world and creating situations where people hurt each other.

"When I was twelve, I took it on myself to find out whether my dad was right or the news was right. I *needed* to know. It turns out neither was anywhere in the ballpark. Chemicals harmed my dad, but not ones that anyone knows about, and there's no way to undo the damage. The U.S. did things, unspeakable things, carried out by men and women who didn't know the harm they were causing. The U.S. as a machine is horrific and systemized in creating destruction. Men make those decisions, but often they're fed inaccurate information. Sometimes the information is incorrect because people get things wrong, and sometimes the misinformation is strategically given to them. Our military–industrial complex is too big to be efficient and is easily swayed to serve those with a hunger for power—"

"You're Doogie Howser with an internet connection," Misha interjected.

Trevor laughed. "Your file doesn't say anything about a sense of humor."

"That's because I don't have one. So, you decided to find out if you could help your dad. That's cool, but I don't deal with computer fraud, kid, so I can't be bothered to take you in."

"I know. You're here because I wanted you here. It's a bit risky, but sometimes one has to take risks. After I found out about what happened and how the government works, I was hooked. I couldn't keep myself away from the information. I wanted to know everything, and then a few months ago, I came across some chatter about you. You're very popular. Did you know you have multiple code names? I personally prefer 'Deicide, the

God Killer', but I think they're going to settle on 'Ubiytsa'. You're a serious threat to the status quo."

Trevor took a few sips of his drink and scanned the room. Misha followed. *Still empty, no bartender even. Oh, there he is. Probably just been out for a smoke.… So, what I'm hearing is that this guy knows things that he shouldn't and that could eradicate U.S. credibility, and he plans to do nothing with this information? He could make Snowden look like a child playing with Minecraft. And in all of his pinging around in the guts of data, he found me. In all the gin joints…*

"I've been an agent for less than a year. There's no way that I have 'multiple code names'."

"I told you that you're interesting. I didn't exactly find you by luck. You're plastered all over the place. That book made it much easier to find the version of you that isn't code-word protected. That was the weakest premise for a bullshit book deal ever. It's obvious that none of it's true, but haven't you ever wondered how the author could get anyone to print it anyway?"

"I figured it's a 'post-facts' era, and the administration wants to crush the 'me too' movement, so needed a wicked woman." Misha cringed, thinking about the book. It hung around like a ghost in the periphery of her thoughts, always ready to jump out and say 'boo.'"

"Sure, that's true. However, some women make Bill Cosby look benign. Think about that for a second. Power corrupts absolutely, and there are women out there with loads of it. So why not go after one of them, instead of a random professor who likes to have kinky sex with her boyfriend? And the most basic Google search can show how wrong the 'facts' are. It's like they didn't even try to make the book plausible."

The shift in the conversation made Misha's skin turn cold. It was fun bantering with this kid, but now he was making her aware of the depth of the setup. Why didn't anyone else suggest this before? Why hadn't anyone tried to help her or acknowledged how weird this situation was?

"That's something I never considered before. I'm aware that no-one cares that it's a lie," she said slowly.

"Ryan Thompson is a douche of the highest order. You, however, aren't the only woman he's encountered. Seriously, though, how on earth did he manage to get your attention? I hope the sex stuff was true, at least—it was kinda hot." His attempt at relieving the intensity of the moment was charming, in a teasingly immature way.

"Erm, not for you to ever know." Misha reached over and tousled his hair. Trevor leaned into it, smiling like this was some joke they'd exchanged before. Misha understood how someone could accidentally tell Trevor things they absolutely shouldn't.

"Fair enough. I don't think you were even the intended target: you were the pawn. This is where the information trail ran a bit thin, and I've had to make some inferences. I suspect that you're similar to a sleeper agent, except that a network surrounds you? And at least one person in that network is of high value to someone who was trying to draw them out, using you as bait. Most of this conjecture, on my part, is from worming into emails up and down the ranks. Does any of this make sense?" He looked at her like she was a physics teacher and he was showing his best attempt at mathematically proving Pythagoras' theorem.

"No, it doesn't—well, at least not yet. But I think I understand what you're trying to describe. I have multiple associates, but I don't know who's trying to use me as bait. Nor do I know who they're trying to draw out." Misha found the thoughts in her mind closing like dusty books and being put back on the shelf. It was one thing to listen to this kid, but it would be quite another to give up names to him.

"So, from what I've read, they didn't understand that.... Do you know anything about the game of chess? Like the basic rules?"

"Sure."

"Okay. Ryan's people thought you were a pawn and an easy way to catch the king. It turns out that you're more like the king, and who they wished to flush out was the queen. You're vulnerable and can only move a little at a time, but you have a fiercely protective queen, and whoever is playing your side of the board knows this game well. Your champion is protecting you with pieces and moves, which are eight moves ahead of Ryan's champion. From everything I've seen, your team has won the game, and all that's left to do is the crying."

Misha thought he must be talking about Max. He was an experienced player. Then again, this kid might not know as much as he thinks he does, and maybe he was talking about Jeff.

"So, why did you want to meet me?" she asked. The safer move was to avoid giving away information or taking more details that led to dead ends.

"You're growing on me, Misha. First, I wanted to meet the person who has everyone all flustered and running around. Second, I don't want to just watch anymore, so I've decided to talk to someone who's in a position to use my skillset. I want to work with you. I think you're moving straight to the top, but you're the underdog. I like people like that."

This observation made Misha laugh from somewhere deep in her belly, and it nearly sounded like a cry as it came out of her throat.

"You doubt this?" Trevor appeared genuinely confused.

"You've seen the napkin. I'm not doing anything good for anyone, including myself." Misha looked down and felt the heaviness of her words. Her ability to create anything positive or meaningful seemed to have disappeared. The thing she wanted more than anything was to have Immie back, but her job made it hard to even be in the same town as her. Trevor was here telling Misha that she was rising to new heights, but all she was doing was avoiding bullets. And who knew how much longer she'd be successful at that?

Trevor leaned back in his chair. "Every time meaningful change begins, things have to shift. No-one enjoys change or hard times, but it's the only thing that leads to growth. What you're currently experiencing are growing pains. I imagine you'll see the dust settle soon. Breathe and keep going. At the rate you're moving, you'll have everything lined up nicely very, very soon."

"Well, that was profound. So you talk about players and chess pieces and growth from change, but you've yet to say any names other than Ryan's. Do you know any other names? Is there a reason you're holding that part back?"

"I don't think that's what you need to know. It might startle you and make it harder for you to do your work if you knew how well protected you are at all times. You aren't even alone in Tulsa. I'm going to tell you two useful things, and then I'll go, to allow you some space to process things. That'll leave you with a couple of days to take in the sights of Tulsa and figure out your next move. Misha, you're doing things well, and I'll be here when you need me because we're going to work together for a long time, Boss Lady. To get where you're going, you'll need to confront Ryan. He has something you need, and once you have that, well, there's nothing to stop you from moving up to the top. The other thing is less clear: find out more about the First Democrats PAC. That comes up a lot in my reading lately." With that, Trevor stood up and left. Misha watched him go and missed him almost immediately.

That was the most normal Misha had felt in a while. Now she needed to decide if Trevor had anything to offer that was useful. And he'd been generous enough to provide a little time to get that sorted. What did Ryan Thompson have, and how would she find it?

Misha's phone buzzed. It was a notification from the dating site she still used occasionally, although she'd stopped messaging the more violent members. This buzz was from a new person: Betamax69. She half-considered deleting the entire app there and then. She didn't need this like she did all those months ago when she was so lonely. Now she had too many real problems to indulge in this sort of activity. She read the text anyway.

The message was short and to the point: "If you need me from now on, you can find me here." Misha texted back, "Thanks." She started to think how Trevor could know she had an account on this site but then realized that could take her down an uncomfortable rabbit hole of acknowledging that there was nowhere on the internet that could keep Trevor out. Instead, she chose to feel comforted that she had an ace in her pocket because she believed what Trevor had told her: that he was an outsider. She finally had someone within her sphere of influence who wasn't put there to nudge her this way or that. She had a friend she could count on for help.

Misha ordered some water. As she sat there, she thought about her conversation on the flight back with Jeff and Max and about what Trevor had told her. Then she looked down at her napkin. Trevor was right: the napkin notes were irrelevant because they represented Misha playing in someone else's game. She didn't need Jeff to fight for her, or Max to guide her, or Trevor to explain things to her. She needed to shift from being an actor in this play to writing the show. It was time to decide what *she* wanted. She was ready for what was coming next, and she wasn't afraid to fight.

CHAPTER 12

"ANYTHING ELSE, OR ARE YOU done?" asked the military official gruffly. Today, more than ever, he wanted out of this stuffy room with these disgusting people. Nothing of consequence ever seemed to happen.

"This one is different from most of the ones we handle, sir. A real pickle. I don't believe we know the full scope of the issue. We'd be deciding in the blind, sir," replied the man with glasses.

The man without glasses coughed and added in a droning voice, "The risks are exposure for most, damage to international reputations for some, direct consequences on the market, the possibility of a government overthrow, and a few unplanned casualties. The opportunity is to maintain the government, gain more funds from multiple Fortune 500 companies, and maintain order." He glared at the man in glasses as if to say, "I've got your blind decision right here."

"What do you think?" the military man asked the table.

The woman replied, "We believe it's a go."

The man with glasses raised his voice in protest. "It's *not* a go, Carol. It's a bad plan, and the tide can no longer be held back with a little glue. We need to open the floodgate to let a little water through, or we may lose the dam altogether. You've tried twice, and twice you've failed. It's time to let a few of them hang in the wind, so that we can all move on."

For a few moments, the people were as quiet as the table.

The man without glasses took a sip from his glass, cleared his throat, and addressing the man with glasses said, "What do you propose, Phillip? A floodgate's often prone to breaking and can't be closed again."

"I propose we burn strategically and give the public their outcry, to provide cover for the rest, which is a damn sight more than any of them deserve," said Philip.

For someone who'd never shown emotion before, the man without glasses looked positively pissed. "Which is it, Philip: a fire or a flood? Pick a metaphor and be consistent. Clarity's paramount in these meetings, and you know it."

"Of course, Joshua. I propose that we destroy Mr. Thompson, a couple of senators, and sacrifice a few celebrities. Their #notmetoo was weak as a plan. I told you, Carol, we couldn't trust this president to do anything by himself. He's useless. I told you all in this meeting that it was a weak plan. Do the tried and true. No-one trusts senators or celebrities, and Mr. Thompson was a nobody before, and he can go right back to it. Getting the office of POTUS cover by trying to make the U.S. in this crazy man's image was a bad, ill-informed plan. We shouldn't double down. Sorry, Joshua, but we shouldn't choose this plan. Is that specific and clear enough for you?" He sat back in a huff.

"Carol?" asked the military man.

"Fine. You spoke your piece, Philip. However, we can't move forward without unanimous agreement. We'll need to decide how we wish to proceed. I need everyone to take out the sealed envelope in the back of their folder on procedures to get to a unanimous decision." Carol paused while everyone did as instructed. Then she began to read out loud, "In case a file is not agreed upon unanimously in the room, persons who dissent may voice their concerns—." She glared at Philip. "Then the team has four options: 1. Discuss until consensus is reached; 2. Delay the item until the next meeting; 3. Return the item to the requester; 4. Kill the breaker of consensus. Once—" Carol was interrupted by the sound of a gunshot as the military man shot Philip right through his newly cleaned glasses. After a brief pause, she continued, "—a decision is settled upon, the team may move this form to the side and continue. If there are any bodies to be removed, press the button in the hall at the end of the meeting."

The three refolded the letters, put them back in the envelopes, and returned them to the back of their folder. Carol, Joshua, and the military man flipped the page and continued their work.

The rest of the meeting progressed in the same way as always. After the three had reviewed the last sheet, they closed their folders and returned them to Carol. The military man handled Philip's folder, somewhat sticky with blood. The three left, and Carol flipped through her portfolio, memorizing the contents. After she'd gone through the papers twice, she took all four folders and walked past Phillip to a hatch next to the door, which had the appearance of a trash chute. She pulled it open, and a fiery glow lit up her face as she dropped the folders into a blaze. She knocked once and opened the door where Joshua and the military man were waiting on either side of the doorway. Carol pressed a large blue button opposite, and then the three of them headed down the corridors, in different directions.

Five minutes later, two gentlemen in hazmat suits with tackle boxes entered the room. Two hours later, after they'd left, the room looked identical to before—everything the same and in exactly the same place. Philip, however, was never seen again. And three blocks away, a chimney in a popular NYC-style pizza place smelled of barbecue.

CHAPTER 13

HARPER WAS CONCERNED. SHE WASN'T sure what to do. Mr. McDougal hadn't been to the office in two days. He was a very private man and didn't take well to people interfering in his personal affairs. As he saw it, when he was in the office, he was in the office, and when he wasn't, he wasn't. But Mr. McDougal usually made at least one appearance a day to discuss what needed to be done, so he didn't understand why his secretary should keep track of his comings and goings, as it wasn't going to change whether or not he was available to take a call. On more than one occasion, he'd told her condescendingly, "I expect you to do your job without interference."

For two years, this situation had more or less worked. The few times Mr. McDougal had asked Harper to come to his office, he dictated his business wants and needs, all the while wiping away faint smudges from his glasses, and she took meticulous notes in her best short-hand. After he'd finished, though, he never told Harper that she was free to go. Instead, he just sat in silence, staring at her, until she understood, excused herself, and left.

Beyond this, Harper relied on her intuition to get by and just hoped she wouldn't lose her job. It was one of the best-paying jobs she'd ever had, and everyone told her that this man could launch her career, or even better, introduce her to a potential husband. He had an impressive track record for losing his secretaries to the sons of the elite, the Fortune 500, the barons of Wall Street. So Harper gave everything she could to the job. Though she knew there was no point in discussing this directly with Mr. McDougal, for he wasn't a fan of being asked direct questions or having his methods explored. All she'd managed to learn about his methods of playing matchmaker had come from her sorority sisters, whose answers were vague statements like, "Well, Todd just showed up in the office one day," or "He gave me an invite to a party he didn't want to go to, and Kevin was seated next to me." This left Harper with the feeling that Mr. McDougal did everything on his own schedule and in his own way. She tried to be patient.

Harper's job wasn't difficult. She arrived at 9 a.m., dressed as if for a garden party—hair and make-up done well enough to be attractive without looking overly eager to please the hosts. She was the image of a debutante with a job. First, she'd check the email inbox and then put on a pot of coffee. Then she'd check voicemail and write all messages on memo pads, including notated pauses and fillers such as "um" or "like," and then put the messages on the edge of her desk. After that, she'd do anything asked of her, which was usually nothing.

Harper wasn't sure what she disliked more: the hours of sitting in an office with no-one to talk to and nothing to do or the always unexpected arrivals of Mr. McDougal, with his imposing presence and unspoken rules. Whenever he was around, Harper felt like she was being disapproved of, as if she were a naughty child. He never told her that she'd done something well, but nor had he ever pointed out her mistakes. He was always looming over the office space whenever he was there. He was more like an annoying ghost than a boss.

A couple of times a month, a man or woman would come in to meet with Mr. McDougal. Even though he didn't keep a schedule book with Harper, he always arrived on time for these appointments, without any assistance from her, other than the coffee she made in the morning. She was always nervous, though, that he'd forget about these meetings, and she'd be left to deal with the visitors herself. Previously, hoping to show herself as someone who takes initiative, she suggested in passing that they both use a Google calendar. For her efforts, she received a look of ice and a repeat of his mantra that they should both do their jobs without oversight from the other. This settled the issue once and for all, and Harper resolved never to mention it again.

So, on this third day of Mr. McDougal's absence from the office, Harper sat at her desk, trying to work out the best course of action. Whom could she call? And what would she say to them anyway? She presumed Mr. McDougal had family somewhere, but his desk was devoid of photos, and as with most things, he was silent on the subject. Even if she had a family member's number, she'd sound rather pathetic: "Hello, do you know anything about Mr. McDougal's whereabouts? He hasn't been to work in two days, which is a bit unusual for him. I want to find out if he's okay, and also, would you mind keeping this conversation to yourself, as he doesn't appreciate prying."

Harper decided to just stick it out for another day at least and get on with her minimal tasks. There were three emails in her inbox. Two were advertisements: for Ann Taylor and Stitch Fix. The third was from Mr. McDougal. In two years, this was the first email he'd ever sent her. Until now, she didn't even know he had an email address, or that his first name was Philip. He'd always signed all correspondence 'Mr. McDougal,' and his few business associates referred to him in the same way. At first, Harper had been curious about his first name but after a while stopped even thinking about it.

Not only was the email itself unusual, so was the request, asking Harper to pull several files for one of his associates. Harper knew that Mr. McDougal's almost desperate need for privacy meant he didn't like her snooping around in his filing cabinets when he wasn't there, so in his absence, she was always careful to confine her tasks to making coffee and checking voicemails and emails. She sometimes wondered if he had hidden cameras in the office, making sure she stuck to the unspoken rules. But she didn't care if he did—she was just there to find a husband who could keep her in the lifestyle to which she'd like to be accustomed, or failing that, improve her career prospects. The cameras would find her utterly without curiosity because nothing in those cabinets was worth jeopardizing her future.

So Harper sat at her computer, contemplating the email. After a while, she concluded it was a test, and one she wanted to pass. So, she resolved to take it very seriously and proceed carefully. She gave herself a few hours to think about any possible pitfalls, since there was nothing else to do. At least there was something to think about.

There were no calls or voicemails to transcribe. There were no visitors. The only sound was the ticking of the clock on the wall. It was like being on a diet, with a cupcake sitting on your desk. Harper preferred any job to waiting for something to happen. Eventually, she crept to Mr. McDougal's office, gently twisted the vintage brass door knob, and eased open the door. The room was imposing—the office of a D.C. mover and shaker. The desk was old, wooden, heaving with ornamental carpentry, and it had a matching chair. Behind this were several barrister bookshelves that framed two mahogany filing cabinets.

Harper felt like she was sneaking in the hall closet to see what

Christmas presents her parents had hidden there. Each of the two cabinets had five drawers. She started from the top left and worked her way down and then over, like reading a book. She'd printed out the list of names given her by Mr. McDougal. The first was "Samuel's Affair."

The first drawer wasn't in alphabetical order. It was filed by numbers and dashes. Harper closed it and went down to the next one, which appeared to be organized by amounts of money in dollars, then pounds, euros, and rubles. *Not that drawer either.*

In the third drawer, there were no files at all: just three boxes that resembled what one would get at a jewelry store. The temptation to open these was immense, but Harper reminded herself that Mr. McDougal would be furious if he found out. She stayed on task and opened the fourth drawer. A quick glance showed her this was probably one of the right drawers, for she recognized a couple of the names as those on her list. Harper reviewed her printout and realized they were not in alphabetical order but in the same order as her list. She pulled the eight required files from the drawer and put them on the center of Mr. McDougal's desk. She placed the email printout on top of the pile and crept out, as if Mr. McDougal were there reviewing the files and she didn't want to disturb him.

She returned to her desk and to nothing to do. Mr. McDougal didn't tolerate cell phone use in the office and required that all cell phones were placed in a cupboard in the hallway before entering. So she went to the internet and searched for entertainment that was suitable for the workplace. Eventually, she reached a point of boredom that even the internet couldn't assuage. She pulled a small journal out of her Louis Vuitton tote bag and began to doodle, presuming this wouldn't incite too much ire if Mr. McDougal were to walk in suddenly.

About an hour before the end of the workday, Harper checked her email one more time. There was another email from

Mr. McDougal. After two years of never sending an email, he did it twice in one day? Very curious. The message was simple: "The courier will be there at six. Have the files ready to go."

This time, Harper walked without hesitation to her boss's office and collected the files and the printed list of names. She parceled up the files to perfection—after all, she had nothing else to do—and checked the labeling at least three times: Samuel's Affair, Thompson Report, Whale Addendum, Benson, Jackal, Senior Constant, Ubiytsa, and Moore. As an afterthought, she took her printed email, placed a check by every one of the documents listed, and placed it in the now-empty filing cabinet drawer.

She cleaned the coffee pot, tidied the clean office, and switched off the lights in Mr. McDougal's office. There was nothing more to do until the courier arrived. She pulled out her journal again and recommenced doodling.

Thirty minutes later, at five o'clock, a beautiful woman in a trench coat arrived. The woman looked about the space as if she was lost. She must be a courier for one of the law firms: *one of the partner's vapid nieces in need of a job.* Harper felt a pang of jealousy that this woman was probably paid more than her to dress pretty and go about the city transferring an envelope here or a package there.

Harper was in the mood to abuse this lost woman out of jealousy, but again, Mr. McDougal would never stand for that kind of behavior from his assistant. At least this woman was earlier than expected, so Harper could leave nearer on time. Harper lifted the package and practically shoved it into the woman's arms.

The courier took it with a puzzled look and then turned and left. Harper was thankful that her day of sitting around wondering about her boss and his strange behavior was over. She grabbed her things, left, and locked the office. She was eager to get home and watch a rerun or six of *Grey's Anatomy* and drink a bottle of white wine to prepare for another tedious day at work tomorrow.

CHAPTER 14

AFTER MISHA'S TALK WITH TREVOR, she returned to D.C. the next day to explore the leads he'd given her. She wanted time alone to work, so she did her best to lose any possible tails from the airport and checked into a seedy motel that was happy to accept cash in exchange for discretion. There she made her plans regarding two tasks: keeping herself alive and exploring Trevor's leads. Misha felt like the two goals were at odds from the start. How does one both hide and walk on the streets of a city covered in spies and informants? It was going to be complicated.

First, she decided to check out the PAC Trevor mentioned over confronting Ryan. However, there was no address listed on Google maps or in Google search. Though the Google search did turn up Democrats First PAC on Open Secrets. Misha looked through the lists of recipients and donors from the PAC. She felt lost at first, but then she took a deep breath and started learning as much as she could about each entity listed. After hours of searching, she started to see some patterns. All of the money spent and given to the PAC was from here in D.C., and certain names kept showing up. That information she took to Google maps and noticed that a high percentage of the organizations and people could be tracked back to a four-mile radius in D.C.

Misha felt it was time to hit the pavement. The area she was going to had a reputation for being occupied and frequented by the powerful elite and their underlings. Misha dressed up for the occasion. Saks would have what she needed for this operation, but that would require her to use one of her credit cards. She reasoned it was worth the risk, knowing that she'd have to work fast and put even more effort into being invisible in plain sight once the credit card was run.

In the early afternoon, a newly attired Misha started walking the area she'd mapped out. An hour later, she passed by an older looking building that had "Democrats First PAC" on the name-plate, along with a few other businesses. Curious, Misha pulled up Google maps to see what businesses were listed on the map. The building was grayed out on Google with the label "U.S. Publishing Government Office." Misha tried the door. It was unlocked. She entered a large foyer and walked along it until she saw a door with "Democrats First PAC" on it. The lights in the office were still on. Misha looked inside. She'd ask for directions to the closest coffee shop as an excuse.

As soon as Misha passed into the office through some type of antechamber, with a lock box and a coat tree, the receptionist pushed a package into her arms. Misha didn't get to look at the office for more than a few seconds but took the package, as it would give her an excuse to return tomorrow. She'd have the night to come up with an excuse for accepting the package.

When she returned to her hotel room, Misha resolved to see what was in the envelope. She hoped there'd be enough to grease the wheels tomorrow to learn more about this organization and what they were doing. But then she couldn't believe what she was reading. Inside the files were intelligence agencies documents that should be "for eyes only," never to leave the reading rooms. She saw no "deliver to" or "in care of" or "we are committing fucking treason—burn if found." And then it hit her in the stomach: she understood what some of these files were about, more specifically who. The Thompson file was a combination of information agencies' reports leading up to and following the publication of Ryan Thompson's tell-all, and the Whale file outlined her work in Budapest and the attempted hit ordered by someone in the U.S. As Trevor had said, her code name was 'Ubiytsa'—an ominous title. Trevor did more than show he was loyal to Misha: his information led directly to Misha getting documents written from the perspective of the people out to get her. She now had data to back up all the stories Jeff, Max, and now Trevor had told her. They were her get out of jail or burn it all to the ground card. Misha now had to entrust them to someone she'd trust with her life.

She trusted Jeff with many things, but he wasn't doing so well at keeping her safe lately. Misha considered Max, but that didn't feel right either. *How could a kid from nowhere Texas find information these two seasoned spies had missed, or was this another secret they were keeping from her?* All three of these men had given her the right information, but none of them had shown her how to get out of her predicament. That's when she knew her answer: there was only one person in her life who could help her with a situation like this.

Misha prepared to go out the second time that day. She leaned heavily into her tradecraft and intuition to make herself as disguised as possible with sweatpants, an oversized hoodie, and some make-up magic.

"Hey, Immie, this is M. New phone," Misha texted with the prepaid cell phone she'd picked up at the third gas station she tried. She wasn't sure that Immie would respond at all, but in less than two minutes, she felt the new phone vibrate in her pocket.

"I. Don't. Care."

"Immie, I need some help with buying an antique," Misha texted back.

"What's it going for?" Immie texted a few seconds later.

"It's a five-thousand dollar lamp. But I'm not sure it's a good deal and was hoping you could give me some advice."

"Send over the information, and I'll let you know."

"Thanks, Immie. I appreciate it." Misha wanted to text more but knew to keep things short.

"Fine. Anything else?"

"No. Thanks."

Misha kept walking as she removed the battery and sim card from the phone and dropped pieces of it down the sewers on the way back to her hotel room.

Misha was thankful that Immie even responded. Although she often sent Misha random and occasionally vaguely threatening texts, she wasn't in the habit of returning messages from Misha. And it didn't help Misha that her work situation meant there were often delays in sending and receiving messages. But after reading the files, she knew there was no-one except Immie whom she could trust. The marriage might be over, but they were family, and Misha felt that Immie would still have her back if push came to shove. She wished she could tell her that they mightn't have time to get a divorce—at this rate, she'd probably be dead soon.

More than this, though, Misha needed someone who knew how to hide things. And Immie was a prepper who hid supplies all over Berkeley, Oakland, San Francisco, Alameda, and San Leandro. Quite possibly, there were stashes of survival gear down in San Jose too, but Misha didn't know for sure: Immie kept some things to herself. When they were dating, Misha sometimes thought about breaking up with Immie over her obsessions with having secrets: systems, spots, and mailboxes all over town. When Misha tried to understand the obsession, Immie was vague. Something about being prepared for earthquakes. Misha didn't believe it. But in the end, she reasoned that the child-like cloak and dagger meets apocalypse prepper was charming. Today, Immie's craziness might even save Misha's life.

Misha was thankful that she'd remembered Immie's secret codes. Immie insisted women needed to have a separate language to alert each other to danger without drawing attention to themselves. On the surface, Misha agreed, but she only used Immie's codes as a way to get out of tedious social situations. Tonight, for the first time in all their years together, Misha used the system for real. "Antiques" was code for trouble, as a text to a friend about antiques was unlikely to raise any concern. The zeros after the price were an explanation of how much fear was involved. Three out of five zeros showed that the situation was not ideal, but she was currently safe. Without making use of that system now, Misha wasn't sure if Immie would stop to listen.

Now Misha took her time walking, crossing, doubling back, and running counter-surveillance maneuvers as she headed back to the dump of a hotel. While walking, she thought about how her life had been orchestrated, and she started to think more about Immie's code. *What was Immie's role in Misha's life? Who was that woman really?* A few weeks earlier, a thought like that would leave Misha feeling vulnerable and hopeless, but now it felt like something else. Possibly it was that emotions like doubt have no place when a person's fighting for survival. Or maybe it was that Misha was feeling more accepting of herself and her ability to succeed against all the odds. If only Misha could share these parts of herself with Immie. If Immie knew the truth, maybe she'd forgive Misha and take her back.

As she neared the hotel, Misha shifted her thoughts back

to the documents hidden in the room and how she'd get them to Immie undetected. In the end, she decided the postal system had email beat. Misha had already identified a run-down shop with a copier, a good place to hide documents, and two separate postal systems to mail the documents to Immie's alternative postal boxes. Anyone could tap into Immie's or Misha's email accounts, but someone would have to be following Misha pretty closely to get one of the documents, let alone all three copies.

Misha was definitely feeling stronger in her craft as she took the long way back to her hotel room. She was exhausted and her feet hurt, but she felt like she was out in front of danger instead of being surprised by it.

CHAPTER 15

HALFWAY THROUGH A CHEAP SAUVIGNON blanc and deep into the sixth season of *Grey's Anatomy*, there was a knock on Harper's door. The junkie college student next door had probably locked herself out of her apartment again. Harper found herself wishing, as she did most days now, that her dream of being married to a guy with a hedge fund and a townhouse had become a reality, and she was far away from this middling apartment with an obnoxious neighbor studying art and oxy on her daddy's dime. "Take that job," her sorority sister had said. "It's the deal of a lifetime." But the deal turned out to be two prime baby-making, spa-living years wasted, sitting mostly alone in a dark office.

Harper put down her Thai takeaway and went to look through the peephole. She was surprised to see not a wasted student but an older woman with a nose like a hawk. This hawk comparison was apt, given the fluidity in the woman's neck as she considered the space around her, like she was looking for prey. The woman was dressed impeccably in a well-fitting black dress and a Chanel jacket and was carrying a large Coach handbag. The look would have been spot on in the 1990s but seemed a bit Halloweenish for the 2010s.

"Uh… hello," Harper said, puzzled. Maybe it was her neighbor's mom coming to ask if Harper knew where her daughter was, or worse, trying to wheedle out information about her. There was nothing about gossip that appealed to Harper, unless it was fiction and involved the cast of *Grey's Anatomy*. Harper wanted to give this woman a piece of her mind. People shouldn't let their children study art and take drugs. When has that ever led to a good marriage?

"Good evening, Miss Hanover. I'm here to inquire after a missing collection of files that my employer was supposed to receive a few nights ago." The woman was cold, her eyes calculating, and her voice firm.

"I'm sorry, but I don't know what you're talking about." This woman was up to no good but was obviously skilled at finding private addresses—there was no way Mr. McDougal would ever have supplied this woman with her address. Harper felt confident that playing ignorant would suffice.

The woman seemed unfazed by Harper's response. "You're Miss Harper Hanover, personal secretary to Mr. Philip McDougal at First Democrats PAC." Harper wanted to point out that her job title was personal *assistant*, but that would have thrown away playing dumb. She wasn't going to be baited into an affirmative response that easily.

Harper continued to study the woman through the peephole in the hopes it would reveal some detail that she could work with to navigate the conversation. If this was work-related, the woman could have come by the office during work hours. Harper was getting annoyed. She wanted to be watching the "Valentine's Day Massacre" episode and forget about the outside world. She had no patience for anyone's bullshit today, but something was warning her to be careful. This woman wouldn't find out anything about

Mr. McDougal or his work from her lips. She'd been keeping secrets nearly all her life, so she was unlikely to slip up now.

"If I *was* someone called Harper, and if I *did* work for someone called Mr. McDonald, I'm sure your problem would be better discussed in the workplace tomorrow. But as I don't know who or what you're talking about, I can't help you. Now, if you don't mind, I have company over—"

"Your name is on your mailbox downstairs. You *are* Harper Hanover." There was no discernible emotion in the woman's voice—she was simply stating a fact.

"You know that someone named Harper Hanover collects her mail at a box in this building, but you need more than that to confirm an identity." *Was that true?* Harper decided it sounded believable, so continued, "You're obviously very committed to your work, making personal calls late at night when you must know that work should be conducted during office hours, at the workplace. So, I suggest you leave now, or I'll phone the police. Good night." Damn it. Harper didn't mean to be polite, but her father had taught her always to show respect.

A tiny smile flickered across the woman's face. "Very well, but please know that those files are highly important to my employer. Someone will collect them tomorrow. If they don't reach their destination this time, I'll be returning, and we'll have a much longer discussion." She turned and walked away slowly, like a tiger walking away from a carcass after filling itself on the kill.

For a second, Harper gave herself over to the chill running up her spine and called after the woman, "What if I hear anything from Harper? How should she contact you?"

"That's not how it works, Ms. Hanover. I contact you, not the other way around." The woman didn't slow her pace or turn back. She let her words float down the hall, with no concern whether

Harper had heard her or not. There was no point in telling the girl that nobody denied Carol information twice.

Her hands shaking, Harper triple-checked her door was locked. What was going on? First, her boss disappears for days at a time, then he sends her emails. And now there was this woman saying that the files had not been delivered, which was ridiculous because Harper had personally handed them to the daft courier in the beautiful coat. If she was incapable of getting the files from one location to another, that wasn't Harper's fault.

Anxiety about what had just happened soon gave way to anger. Why should she have to deal with a horrible, rude woman coming to her home about work matters? Harper made up her mind to give Mr. McDougal an ultimatum: introduce her to a young man this month, or she'd quit and find a husband herself.

But then Harper's logical thoughts took over. There really was no way that woman should know where she lived. Her hands began to shake again. She needed to protect herself, and the person who could best help her to stay safe was the person she trusted the most, her father.

Before she phoned her father, though, she tried to mentally compartmentalize what she knew about her employer and his business, to make sure she didn't relay anything that would compromise either Mr. McDougal or her father. Once she'd established clear partitions in her mind, she picked up the phone.

"Daddy?"

"Hello, Baby," General Hanover bellowed. "It's late for you to be calling."

Despite having the call all mapped out, the sound of her father's voice drove Harper to tears. Shuddering, she said, "I need your help…. Please come and get me… please, Daddy—"

"Slow down." General Hanover switched instantly to the

stern, focused commander who could lead precision forces. "Tell me what's happened."

"It's about work." Harper took a deep breath to try and stop her sobbing. "Well… a woman came to my door…. My boss has disappeared… and I don't think I'm safe." Harper sank onto the couch and curled into a protective ball, as if she expected the woman to return and break the door down. "Oh, Daddy, please come and get me, now!"

"Baby, I think your brother is on your side of town. I'm texting him now. Don't hang up."

"Thanks, Daddy. I'm so scared. Something is wrong, but I don't know what it is."

"It's okay, Harper. We'll figure it out." General Hanover paused for a moment. "John will be at your door in five minutes. He'll use the special knock. Can you get to your bag?"

Part of having a father in the military meant Harper and her three brothers had been taught to keep a personal mobility bag. But since their mother died, the boys had become so protective of Harper—basically providing her with her own personal three-man army—that she'd felt confident enough to let some of her father's lessons and protocols slide, including the go-bag thing.

"Sure, Daddy. Grabbing it now," Harper said as she rushed to find where she'd hidden the bag last year and update it with essentials for hiding out at her father's. If he heard her mad scrambling, he didn't call attention to it. Instead, he talked to her and tried to calm her with techniques straight from the battlefield. As she listened, Harper was wondering if she could manage with just two handbags. Settling on the addition of a clutch too, she stuffed them all in the bag, along with her make-up, and grabbed her purse. She sat back on the couch, and as if on cue, her brother knocked on the door.

As soon as Harper let him in, John began to assess the

apartment. Checking for a safety breach was the level of overkill that her brother used to demonstrate how perfect a son he was. Although Harper didn't know why he bothered, as she was the obvious favorite, she was secretly thankful for his wish to keep her safe, which was how he showed his love for her.

He took Harper's phone. "Sir, the apartment is clear. We'll be there at 21:35."

"Good work, John."

He hung up and led Harper to the safety of his car.

CHAPTER 16

SIPPING AN AMERICANO, MISHA WATCHED through the café window as yellow and orange leaves fell to the ground. She set down her iPad and gazed at the bridge over the Seine. Prior to flying to Paris, she'd submitted her heavily doctored report on Trevor Hill and then waited in D.C. for her next assignment. So far, there'd been no hint that anyone knew about her and the files: she'd decided not to tell Jeff and Max. If she was honest with herself, it felt good to have this with Immie alone. Some couples try to reconnect over ballroom dancing or playing cards, but Misha was discovering that hiding top-secret files with her wife was rekindling something in Misha's heart.

Last week, Immie had sent coded texts to confirm that she'd received the package and that she'd see Misha at the meetup location next week. Misha had a chance to sit face-to-face with Immie and maybe change their trajectory.

Meanwhile, Jeff swore to Misha that she'd be safe in Paris, and that this was just a tedious task that required her to perform a series of functions. Nothing more complicated than that. However, he'd missed the assassination attempt in Budapest and the hacker kid in Tulsa, so Misha wasn't feeling optimistic about his ability to sniff out danger. He'd looked so sincere though, and Misha wasn't inclined to tell him that he was fucking up his job—they were friends, after all. Maybe this was as good as spy handlers get, given that they worked in espionage, where everyone was a trained liar with questionable motives. Things often weren't cut and dry. Misha decided it was best to think like a spy from now on and believe that she couldn't trust anyone. That way, she couldn't be disappointed when horrible things happened. It also left Jeff feeling confident about his role, and from Misha's perspective, a confident handler who was mediocre at spotting danger was still better than a cranky best friend who'd given up.

For a moment, Misha allowed herself to focus on the joy and hope in seeing Immie again. Hope was dangerous when one's life was at stake, but without it, there wasn't much value in life anyway. Misha imagined Immie here with her, drinking coffee and laughing happily, and longing grew inside her. Forcing herself from this reverie, Misha saw her asset ordering at the counter. Time to get back to work.

Misha grabbed her cup and plate, threw her iPad into her bag, and walked toward the counter. A foot from the asset, she tripped, and her cup and plate crashed to the floor. This always reliable "accident" allowed the asset to bend down to help clear up the mess. Misha opened her satchel, pulling out a napkin "to mop up the spilled coffee," but under cover of the confusion, he dropped something small in her bag. Misha quickly took more napkins from the counter, and together they picked up the broken cup and plate and gave the floor a cursory wipe. Then, with perfect American loudness, Misha apologized in broken French and left the café, seemingly flustered.

Once out of the eye-line of the café, Misha picked up her pace along the river, doing a few crosses and trying to spot any similarities among her fellow pedestrians. Never content with her evasion skills, she added in a few additional passes. She then headed to an assigned apartment. From here, there was time and the tools for two hours of analysis, memorization, encryption, surveillance, and a clothing change. When the work was completed, Misha slipped the USB into a heel of her new boot, put on a Givenchy blazer, and slipped out a different way than she'd entered. She was off to meet with a publisher friend, Jeff's cover story for the mission, to discuss writing her own story, as a contradiction to the narrative that had destroyed her career as a professor.

As Misha and the publisher finished their coffee, Misha gave her "friend" the coded phrase, "Thank you for the consideration, but that book was ages ago, and I have a good job now that enables me to afford beautiful things, like these boots."

"Oh, no. Are they new?" the publisher said in Parisian-accented English.

"Yes, why? What's wrong with them?" Misha leaned down, napkin in hand, to look at her boots, and with the napkin for cover, quickly removed the USB from the heel.

"Oh, I see. It was just a smudge. Well, I must return to the office."

"Yes, of course. Thank you for joining me for coffee. It's been too long." Misha hugged her friend, slipping the USB in her pocket in the process. The second step of the day's mission was complete.

Today was a great day to be a spy—in Paris, with perfect weather. So much better than days spent walking in freezing rain or having groups of agents following her every move. She was a known operative in France. There should be at least one tail at one point in the day. Misha was surprised that there was no-one to evade, but maybe they didn't care about what she was there to do, or there were more dangerous spies in the country? Nothing was wrong necessarily, but Misha took note of how easy the day was going and reviewed tradecraft tips and tricks in her mind to prepare for a range of possibilities. She did some extra passes through neighborhoods and arrived at lunch a few minutes later than anticipated but still early enough to get a table with her back to the wall and a clear view of the room and the street. The lunch date was as expected. It was a simple check-in with the head of the operation in Paris. He confirmed what Misha already knew: no-one was following her, and all was going well. Misha headed off for her fourth and final stop of the day, College de France, to meet with some neuroscientists for a paper Jeff was writing on machine learning. Misha made a mental note to talk to Jeff about over-scheduling her. If anything had gone wrong, she wouldn't have been able to compensate appropriately. Four stops in eight hours barely left enough time to clear each scene and maintain cover. If she had a tail who was experienced in counter-evasion techniques, getting to the next stop could have taken many hours.

With the working day done, Misha could now relax. During Misha's sophomore year of high school, Misha's mom had sent her to work as an au pair for her old college roommate, who was then the ambassador to France. The children Misha looked after were now college students, and she'd arranged to meet up with them in a restaurant. The good company and wine helped push away the duties of the day for a few hours at least.

When Misha finally returned to her room, there was the email she was expecting from "her mother" about how the dogs were chasing squirrels happily. She breathed out with relief: the mission had been a success.

Misha rewarded herself by looking through her dating site, more specifically to re-read an old fantasy from the guy with a penchant for spanking. She told herself there was no threat of exposure if she had her phone on airplane mode and wasn't sending any new messages. She made herself comfortable on the bed, phone in hand. Then, reading the old message, she began to forget all about the stressors in her life. It wasn't long before she was lost in the fantasy, reveling in the details. Then just as she got to her favorite bit, her phone rang. It was Jeff. She'd have to answer.

"Misha! What the fuck! You know I need the notes from your meeting at College de France. Where the fuck are they?" Jeff's tone convincingly wrestled between anger and panic. "You know I need those memos for annotations to my presentation on Friday."

"Tomorrow isn't Friday in Paris or D.C. You're fine," Misha replied.

"I need time to work them into the presentation and to update the slide deck. You're such a disappointment. That's what I fucking get for giving a job to a friend. I feel like I'm paying for this shit every single day. No wonder you aren't a professor anymore—"

"Too far," Misha interrupted.

"I need the annotations by noon in Paris, or you don't have a job when you get back." Jeff hung up.

So, something *was* wrong about that lovely, perfect Paris day after all. Misha knew that it had been too quiet and smooth. No hiccups were often just as bad as too many complications. Jeff's call let her know that she needed to go to their secondary location at noon and find out what had gone wrong.

Misha tried to get back into her smutty fantasy, but the moment had passed. She attempted to sleep instead, but her mind was reeling over what the issue might be. Eventually, she managed a few hours of light sleep, until the rays of morning light shone through the thin curtain into the bedroom.

Despite her tiredness, she started early. She'd be methodical in her technique today and allow plenty of time for absolute thoroughness on her way to the communications checkpoint. She dressed with care and mentally prepared her cover, reviewing and elaborating on details. It was almost a game, the way she tested herself in every aspect.

After hours of picking her way through the city and stopping along the way for a croissant and coffee, Misha slid into the bluish-teal double doors of the hotel and bookstore. She walked up to the cashier and said a name. The cashier handed her a key. Misha ran up the stairs and into the hotel room. This was a safe room, with a secure line and sound-blocking technology. Misha sat on the bed, picked up the phone, and dialed Jeff's secure number. While she waited for him to answer, she ran her fingertips along the book spines of the headboard-come-bookshelf.

Jeff's voice eventually came on the line. "Hello, Mish."

"I'm here."

"Sorry about last night, but I needed you to be careful today."

"You got the point across."

"Good. The publisher made it to the press and got the corrections filed but not back to her office." They were using a secure line, but Jeff was still talking in code, so Misha followed.

"So the paper went to print, but she never got home?" Misha clarified that the flash drive made it to the correct destination before the agent disappeared.

"That's correct. I saw the article this morning. I also believe you got enough notes, and it's now time to come home. I've booked you on a flight at six."

"If you're sure you have enough for your presentation?"

"More than enough. See you tomorrow, bright and early."

"Okay, Boss." Misha hung up. She resumed running her fingers along the book spines, absentmindedly reading the names to herself while she tried to absorb the new mission: get out of Paris alive. Yesterday was all fun and games. Today she was playing Frogger. She thought about how she'd have to study every face and object for threats while she worked her way back across the city and out to the airport. Once she had a mental map prepared for her route out of danger, she quietly left the room.

As she walked from the stairs toward the front of the store to return the room key, something caught her eye. Standing in front of the second row on the left, flipping through a book, was Mr. X. Her muscles tightened involuntarily, as if her body was telling her it was time to run. Here was a definite obstacle. But then she figured that maybe this was a good thing. After all, there were no challenges yesterday, and an asset had gone missing. If Mr. X was the threat, Misha wasn't concerned about her ability at successfully getting out of Paris. She'd already survived him once. Misha's mental math kept saying it was best to make contact because this wasn't a coincidence, and she wanted to know if he had anything to do with the publisher's disappearance.

"Hello, Mr. X. Fancy meeting you here, of all places." Misha kept her voice even.

"Ms. Campbell… every lover could be brought to trial as the murderer of his own love." He didn't lift his eyes from the page.

"You don't beat around the bush, do you?" Misha studied him.

He finally looked up at her. "It's a line in this book. What did you think I was talking about?"

His cavalier attitude raised her ire. "I hope you're feeling better. The last time I was meant to see you, you didn't show up. You had a cold?" There was no need for her to say more about how that night went. He knew: it was in his eyes.

"Oh, I'm fine. Have you ever read this?" He showed Misha the book, *The Four-Chambered Heart* by Anais Nin, and then rolled it back and forth in his palms as if he really wanted advice on whether to buy it.

He looked good, and he was playing it beyond cool. This was

extremely annoying. She was trying to work out the best way to respond. If she left, she couldn't afford to have him at her back, especially if there were other spies outside—she'd be surrounded. But every minute she stayed in this conversation increased the chances of becoming a target. Misha needed to keep moving until she was safely out of Paris. She kept the conversation going to see if it yielded anything. But first she set her mental clock. In five minutes, with or without answers, she was out the door and on her way.

"Yes, I have." She let out a giggle that was only partially forced.

"Why are you laughing?" Mr. X's voice raised slightly, contradicting his above-it-all expression.

"Oh, sorry. It's just that the last time I read it—never mind." Misha changed her mind about sharing memories of reading Nin at college. They weren't ever going to have *that* kind of friendship.

"I've read it before too." He looked down at the book almost bashfully. "I'm sorry I didn't turn up that night, but it isn't what you think. You're important, but there's another…" He paused, his eyes still on the book. "And… this other woman, she has *real* power. But I'm afraid it's all in the past now." He looked Misha in the eye. "That's the best I can do at an apology." Then he handed her the book, kissed her briefly on the cheek, and rushed out of the shop.

Misha flipped through the book and saw handwritten notes. She looked at the gap on the shelf left by the removed book. Sitting between *Delta of Venus* and *Henry & June* was a business card. Misha grabbed it. It was for Nolinski Suites Champs-Elysées and had a number written on the back: probably the hotel room number. She slid it into her pocket. She knew she should tear it up, but fuck it. This conversation was probably a ruse, and if he left the card, then he wanted to have a longer conversation. She flipped through some of the other books on the shelf and saw that *Delta of Venus* also contained notes in the same handwriting. She would purchase it, along with the book Mr. X had handed her, in case he wanted to use some type of book code. There was no way that Misha could go to the hotel, back to the bookstore, and to the airport on time.

Misha paid the person at the register and handed over her key. The terrifying part of her day was now beginning: making it to the airport in one piece. She left the store. There was no-one out front. Misha took a deep breath and set out through the streets. Each blind angle made her heart pound, but this was part of the job. Why didn't the movies ever show James Bond repeating in his head, "Please don't let me die today"? Misha felt like Fleming misrepresented what it meant to be a spy, maybe to encourage young men to line up and join the future clandestine efforts of Great Britain. Misha wished she had some Fleming magic today, so all she had to do was fuck a beautiful woman, drink a Vesper, and take a beating. This thought was a welcome distraction to a mind threatening to fill with the noise of fear.

It was impossible for Misha to know who the aggressors were. So she breathed deeply and scanned for patterns. Her brain was likely to pick up a problem before she consciously noticed any-thing, so she gave herself over to the best parts of her mind: the pattern trackers and reptilian lobe that cared only for survival.

Misha zigzagged ten blocks and took a cab. She was supposed to say she wanted to go to the airport. Instead, she said the name of the hotel. It was a risky move, but her job was a series of risks. A missing agent in the field was a grave danger for every spy in the vicinity, so much so that Jeff had called her back home. But Misha's hunch was that Mr. X had actionable information, and an opportunity like this might not present itself again.

Misha took the elevator up to the sixth floor of the hotel and then took the stairs down to the fourth, along the corridor to the stairs on the opposite side of the building. She went up to the fifth floor. All three levels appeared empty, although this was highly unlikely. Misha didn't notice anything suspicious. She walked along the empty hall. She knocked on the door that matched the number on the back of the business card, standing to the side of the door and holding her breath as she waited for a bullet to tear through the door.

Mr. X. opened the door. He beckoned Misha in, and she sat down at the table, facing the window. Mr. X hadn't killed her in the bookstore, en route, or in the hallway, and she hoped that the trend of not being murdered would continue.

"I wasn't sure you'd come, after the trouble in Budapest."

"Is that what you call a hired hit: 'trouble'?"

He flinched and went to take the seat across from her.

"Close the curtains." Misha pushed her chair back until it was in front of the bathroom doorway. The angle should provide her some cover if anyone came through the door unexpectedly.

Mr. X complied. Now only a sliver of light entered the room, through a gap between the curtains. He turned on a bedside lamp and joined Misha at the table. Without looking at her, he began, "I liked you a lot. More than most. I hadn't felt for anyone the way I felt when I was with you. Ryan is a raving idiot, but now I can't blame him for being devastated. You're like a lightning storm and a tornado all in one. Is there anyone on your level? But there are other… *requirements* for me, and I have more than myself to protect now. I do as I'm told." He shook his head. "This isn't coming out the right way." He faced Misha. "Do you want water? I want water."

Misha glared at him.

He grabbed water from the fridge and returned to his seat. "I am… glad… you aren't dead."

"So am I, and I'd like to stay that way. Do you intend to try killing me again?"

"No, but..."

Misha could see he was getting very agitated. All parts of her mind were telling her to get out of this room, now, but she wasn't going to leave until she learned something, anything, that could be useful.

After a long pause, he continued. "I don't know if I can trust you, but I'm still alive. So thank you for that." He looked at Misha again, and this time, he seemed so vulnerable, like a young boy.

Misha wondered what he was so afraid of that he'd put himself in a position where he preferred risking his life with her than with someone else. What he said suggested that he thought she was here to exact revenge rather than information. Yet he picked this hotel, and they were both here under his terms. For him, the situation was as safe as it gets in this line of work.

Mr. X continued, "This is far more complicated than Budapest or you versus me. We're pawns in a much bigger game. We do what they tell us. I tried to get out. I pulled every string, but she isn't going to let go. It's obvious you don't know your role yet. I wanted to warn you that night in Budapest, but... she... she would've known if I even tried. We all have our parts to play, right? It wasn't personal. I shouldn't be here now, but I met someone, and I don't want to start something with this hanging over my head. I'm sorry I didn't protect you, but you have to leave me alone. I'm out."

Misha had no clue what he was trying to tell her. He was getting more and more frantic and was rambling. She wanted to ask him questions but knew it would interrupt his outpour of information. Her best shot was to listen a moment longer and hope he said something she could use.

"You're untouchable. I had no clue that people like you even existed. I didn't know any of this. I thought you were sexy and lonely and sad. When I got the order, twice, I couldn't ignore it. We had fun, though, right? If they ask, you'll say I was harmless. Please, Mish." He was hugging himself and crying like an inconsolable child. "I love her, and I want out. I thought I was out. Please let me alone. I don't want any trouble."

"Tell me what you know," Misha whispered. What happened to him that had left him so shaken? And why did he think *she* had anything to do with it? He was the one who'd left her for dead, not the other way around.

"I don't know much, Misha. I know that I should have never met you. You're going to destroy everything I love. You're going to kill us all."

"Explain—"

"I can't. You're above reproach. You'll destroy us all. Misha, please help me. Please tell them I didn't do anything wrong. Can you protect me from *her*?" He stood up, rushed next to her, and dropped to his knees. His face seemed to suddenly lack any color. His terror was palpable.

"But I don't know who to tell. How can I help you? Please tell me." Misha lowered her face until it was a few inches from his and squeezed his arm gently in an attempt at reassurance. "I don't know what's happened to you. I have nothing planned that involves you. Please tell me what you know. Maybe I can help."

"You didn't send me these?" He jumped to his feet and rushed over to the bedside table. He tossed postcards in Misha's direction, but they fell to the floor. "I did what I was told to do. It was you or me and mine."

"I'm telling you that I'm here as a result of information you gave me, and I don't know what you're talking about." Misha hoped the sincerity in her voice would bring him around.

"Right. You're so much better than the rest of us." Mr. X

looked around the room as if he was trying to remember where he left his keys. "They don't let agents like me go off-book. But I left after that. I've been to the beach, and I met someone. I'm ready to leave it all behind. Please let me."

"Why do you think I'd be interested in you? I'm in Paris on business that doesn't include you, unless you know where the publisher is?" Misha decided it was time to redirect the conversation.

"What publisher? I was sent to Budapest from London to win your trust and then get out of the way." His expression changed to one of contempt. "Don't act like you didn't know."

"But I didn't."

Sighing, Mr. X walked over to the curtain and peeked through the narrow gap. "Fine. We'll play the game for posterity, Max." Or at least the last word sounded like "Max," before the explosive sound shattered the glass and Mr. X fell back. Misha watched him transform into a red mess on the floor.

For the second time that day, Misha let her body take over. She dropped to the floor, lunged for the postcards, and crawled to the door, staying clear of the sliver of visible window.

Opening the door while on her knees, Misha was relieved to find no-one in the hall. She ran. And kept running. She was half a mile away before she had a conscious thought: she needed to to get to her flight and get out of here. Now that Mr. X was dead too, she was desperate to make the plane before anyone connected her to Mr. X's death.

She stopped in the middle of the sidewalk and looked at her phone. There was still time to make her flight, but it would mean catching a cab and going directly to the airport, which would make her movements easy to follow. But it was her best option.

When she told the cabbie that she was running late, he drove like he was qualifying for the Grand Prix. She made it. The ticket waiting for her at the counter was first class, and she got the fast-pass treatment onto the plane, which must have been Jeff's doing. As she slid, exhausted, into her seat, a tear rolled down her cheek. She didn't think she'd be able to hold back the floodgates, so she mitigated the risk. She got a gin and tonic, chose a romantic film to watch, and put on her headphones—she'd just blend in as a drunk woman, teary-eyed over a romantic production. No-one needed to know that she'd just watched a man get shot in the head in front of her, or that the last thing he said was her boss's name.

Later, she would take her bag into the bathroom and read the postcards, away from the prying eyes of fellow passengers. But first, she'd give herself an hour to cry everything out and enjoy her drink, uninterrupted.

CHAPTER 17

IT WAS QUIET IN THE shop—a dark, rainy Wednesday can do that to any business—so Max decided he'd send Jonathan home and close up early. Jonathan didn't approve of leaving before Max, or of anything for that matter, but Max gave him a stern look, so Jeff shuffled off. Now the store stood dark and silent, reflecting the damp, heavy night through its dark, vacant windows.

Max retreated to his office, the only place where he felt at peace. He settled at the desk that dominated the room. He listened to the sound of wood against wood as he opened the drawer on the left-hand side and slid out a hidden drawer. He removed a pen and a folio of paper and sat down to write out his thoughts. He flipped through the folio to find a blank sheet of paper, pausing once or twice to peruse previous writings.

The phone on an adjacent table rang three times before an answering machine played a short message of Jonathan's voice: "Seriously, a tape recorder? Leave a message, and if this thing works in the morning, we might return your call. Beep." Max listened with mild interest. A voice then said, "Max. I need your help. Things are… I need to talk to you, Max, with a problem. I need a… and it has to be the right one… Max…" The caller sounded sad or maybe resigned as they said the last "Max" before hanging up. Max recognized the voice. It was Misha. He turned his attention back to the papers on his desk.

For nearly forty years, this desk and this drawer had provided a refuge when the world was being challenging. These sheets of paper had been a life raft from terrifying memories. He settled into the ritual of writing down his thoughts in the trance-like way he did when he was unsure of the next course of action. But as he sat there with the linen paper underhand and the scratched Montblanc fountain pen, nothing happened. He just stared ahead. In addition to what was in his line of vision, he pictured the room behind him. He could see into each drawer, and he could feel all the secret compartments. This room held all of him: his past, his work, the terrible memories, and the leftovers from others' actions. He stood, went to one of the drawers in the wall, and felt around for a secret compartment above the drawer. He then removed a Cubano peso held inside and placed it on his desk. Finally, he could concentrate.

Holding the pen in his left hand, he began to write:

September 23

Dear Misha,

This is the third installment of the letter I have been writing to you. I'm still not satisfied; let's see if this addition works better. Maybe I'll give you this stack of papers one day and let you sort out through all of my ramblings. Though I have told you enough to help you get by since Berlin, it seems to me I owe you more.

I started writing to you before you were exposed; it was the first letter I wrote. Then I wrote you another when you went to the Farm and became an agent. But it was too hard to give them to you. In a way, telling you everything feels a little like giving up on the idea that you still need me.

Last, I wrote to you about the invasion of the Bay and how I failed my friends and allies. I wrote about how I was back in the CIA office after going through the photos and identifying the dead as best I could, with the hope of identifying all the tios y primos we lost. I have shown you the hopes and dreams of a nation through my small lens. But again, I digress. At this point, it is relevant to tell you why I have done the things I have and about the foibles to which I have succumbed.

The CIA perpetuates the myth that our agents are the best and the brightest—perfect in every way. Having trained at the Farm, you probably noticed that is not true. We don't want the best or the brightest: we want the arrogant and the strong. Ours is a machine that must give the impression of such grandeur that you will think we will run like clockwork for the next 1000 years. To do this, we need people who will pledge allegiance to whatever we say and are vain enough to do so at all costs. We are all cogs, or as a man I drank with one night famously said, "bricks in the wall." Indeed, I have spent a number of my years making very excellent walls out of very obedient, impressive bricks. Those bricks have taken mortar and bullets and suffered torturous ends because their vanity will continue into spectacular death scenes, if I or someone else calls for it.

I know I have written about it before, but it is very much on my mind tonight. When the Boardroom began, it was a sort of conference of great thinkers with sizable dreams and matching egos. We were not unlike our CIA contemporaries in believing we could solve everything through our plans. But my intent was sincere: I hoped I could make life something of so much value that it would be painful to lose it for one mission or one objective. I meant to make humans so useful that the government would regret even considering letting one die. I was convinced, as young men are about their half-cocked ideas, that my dreams would make the world a better place for humanity.

I didn't realize I had the power to make people live and die with my plans. This is something you need to understand. You must realize that I was trying to fix a system. I did not mean to make new casualties, but I now see the error in my ways—as only an older man can.

My career had been spent working as a spy. I had been taught and influenced by people who fought, killed, and manipulated others. Naively, I thought I could escape that legacy and make something completely new, but that wasn't possible—I was tainted. So I tried to influence each of you gently and keep myself away from you so I couldn't make you sick with my brand of war-hawking. I believe in the work I have done with this program: I think it is excellent craftsmanship. Each of you are brilliant in your skillsets. I am especially proud of you and I have loved you like you are my daughter. When your mother sent me updates or little things like a picture you had drawn, I'd hang it on my fridge.

Because I have loved you so dearly, I need to tell you now that I lied to you. I know who wants to eliminate you, but there is no way that you are ready to face her yet. I've tried to buy you some time. I used Mr. X as a pawn, it was the best way to distract her from you for a while. But she killed him. She tried to kill me once, poison me like the Communists she so admires. I told the team that she spent too much time in Moscow House, but they were happy with her intel.

Did you ever hear about Ana Montes? She sent top-secret information to Cuba using a radio she kept in a shoebox? The woman who is after you to get to me made Montes who she was. Carol got to her. I got to Montes—through intermediaries, as we do. Carol and I have been fighting for years over the best way to lead, a continuous tit-for-tat process using known combatants. Then interest in my program grew, and she didn't like that. I'm still not sure how she found you and is unable to reach the others. I'm sorry you are in this Misha, but I will do my best to get you out, if I'm not too late.

I want to tell you what is coming and how you have ended up in this position. I'm afraid—

A light began to pulse in the corner of the room. Max put down his pen, looked at his watch, and nodded. He returned the pen to its drawer and opened a drawer on the other side of the desk, from which he took out a table lighter and an ashtray, with the care of a priest handling a relic. He placed these objects on either side of his writing but put the ashtray back in the drawer. With admiration, he turned his attention to the lighter, running his fingers over the initials delicately inscribed there: "P.J.G." It was a gift from his first mentor in the agency, who insisted it had belonged to Goebbels. But back then, when there was still so much Nazi paraphernalia around, it was impossible to be sure. Max was sure that his mentor valued and loved him deeply; it was that level of selfless love Max had hoped to surround Misha with before Carol got involved.

Max rolled up his letter to Misha and set it alight with his lighter. Leaving the letter to burn on the table, he lit the stack of pages, dropping sections of it in different locations around the room. As each area took fire from the pages, the office soon became a tinderbox. Time to leave.

The light in the corner blinked again before the power in the room went out. Even without power, the room was bright with the colors of flames burning fuchsia, green, and gold. The beautiful antiques ignited like giant matches. The desk was an inferno, with two objects highlighted in the brilliant blaze: a table lighter and a '58 Cubano peso.

As the fire burned bright, a handful of people dressed in black gear and carrying guns were attempting to batter down the door. This was almost impossible, as the door was made of steel, painted to look like wood. Another group tried to enter the room from the window on the other side but found it equally problematic to penetrate, as the window was bulletproof. The heat from the inferno started to spread to the surrounding vicinity. The two groups gave up and left. They could see there was no chance at successfully completing their mission.

Max had disappeared without a trace.

CHAPTER 18

Misha sat back in Caldera at the same table, staring out the same window. Everything was still sticky, but now it seemed welcoming, like finding fresh jam on a counter. The alcohol was still antiseptic in strength. She could smell the spirits as the glass rested on the table. She pictured herself being baptized in the liquor and how it would pour over her and everything in the bar, removing the built-up residue of history, good and bad, sending all regrets and discretions washing out the door and onto the street.

Working on her second drink, Misha lost herself in fantasies of how this meeting with Immie would go. Waiting was not one of her strengths, so it was a struggle to stay here, praying that Immie would arrive with the promised files. Misha had had to survive so much to be with Immie again. She was giddy with relief. The stakes had been getting higher with Mr. X's death and Max's shop burning to the ground, her champion gone and presumed dead. She kicked back the rest of her drink to dispel unwelcome images of bloody carpets and charred beams crushing waterpipes and replaced such images with a vision of Immie in the trunk of a car. She shook her head and told herself firmly that Immie was just running late and that everything was fine now. Better than fine—any second now, Immie would be within touching distance.

Tonight, Misha was going to stop at these two drinks, or possibly just one more. She had to remain fresh to handle this conversation with Immie. It was an opportunity to show her that she still had something to offer.

Misha saw blonde hair coming up the stairwell to the loft and heard herself exhale over the bustle of the Saturday night crowd. Immie had arrived safely.

Immie sat opposite Misha and arranged herself like she was blocking for a play. She didn't acknowledge Misha as she busied herself with the placement of her coat, handbag, and drink. It was only when she had everything as she wanted it that she looked directly into Misha's eyes. For a moment, she didn't betray any emotion. But then she smiled in a sympathetic way, with real warmth.

"So," Immie said. "We ought to discuss… things."

"I don't know where to start. Is everything safe? Are *you* safe?" Misha hadn't felt this vulnerable in a long time. Her eyes teared up, and her voice caught in her throat.

"I'm fine…." Immie paused. "Everything is as expected and secured. I didn't bring the files with me, but I took the liberty to read up before coming."

"So, you're a spy, too, right?" Misha sounded more accusatory than she'd intended.

"Sort of. I don't do what you do though. I work in a different department." Immie's voice was calm, and her eyes sparkled at the hint of a joke.

"Good. That means you can keep yourself safe." Misha sat back, believing this was a decent recovery from the last statement.

Immie smiled with her mouth, but not with her eyes. "Yes, I'm good at taking care of myself."

"How good are you at taking care of yourself? Good enough that Jeff wanted you to take care of me too?" Misha looked down at her hands as she waited for Immie to tell her the truth. It wasn't the best move forward, but that was what she wanted to know more than anything.

Misha was taken off guard by Immie's giggling. "You are the most insecure person I've ever known," said Immie. "Everything about your life has changed, you send me those documents, and all you want to talk about is my work history?" Immie's cheeks reddened. She was melting under Misha's show of emotion. "Jeff didn't tell you about me? Or rather you were too afraid to ask, coward."

Immie's playful tone wasn't enough to take the sting out of "coward," and Misha flinched. Instantly regretting her poor word choice, Immie said, "My job was to keep you safe,

Mish. I needed to keep you alive, unharmed, and protected from danger. I may have taken a few liberties with my assignment…" Immie giggled, thinking about that first night, when Misha was so dead sexy that she couldn't help but take her home.

The gleam in Immie's eyes matched the sincere smile around her mouth. She held out her hand and rested her fingertips against Misha's hand. Misha was so relieved that their relationship wasn't all a sham.

"But the marriage was real? That part wasn't an assignment?"

"It was our choice. Jeff didn't like it, but he accepted us and smoothed things out up the chain of command." Immie understood that it must be hard for Misha to figure out what was "real" and what was fabricated.

"And now?" Misha's voice trembled. But she kept her questions short to hide her emotions.

"I don't know, Mish. Things were bad. You left—"

"You told me to go," Misha interrupted.

"I said to go and see your best friend. I told Jeff you were spiraling, and he said he'd help talk you down. He's always been better at that than me. I would have never sent you to become an agent." Irritation increased in Immie's voice. Again, she saw Misha flinch at her harsh tone. This wasn't the conversation Immie wanted to have. Her frustration was at the situation, with Jeff, and with her own confusion about the relationship—not with Misha directly. Immie made herself a promise before she got here to not jump for the fight. Not everything that had gone wrong was Misha's fault, and for the first time they could have a real conversation without Immie needing to maintain a partition between her assignment and her relationship with Misha.

"What now, Immie? I did become an agent. I'm different now."

"Are you? You look like Misha." Immie could hear her tone level out. She gently tickled the back of Misha's hand with her fingertips until Misha looked up. "We have some things to figure out. I don't know what happens after that, but I'm... curious.... I want to see if... I don't know. What about you?" It was hard to let Misha off the hook entirely, but there was plenty of blame to go around.

"I want you. I think about you a lot, and I trusted you with the files. But now that we're here, I can't help wondering what is this? I wanted any reason to sit with you and to see if we could make things work again. Now that we're here, I realize I don't know who we ever were to each other. The story about us is completely different for you. All those threats about selling the house or wanting a divorce: do you want that, did you want that, or were they things you said because of some script Jeff gave you?" Misha took a deep breath. So many times she'd tried to talk to Immie, but she never found the right words. Finally, she said something that felt as close as possible to what she wanted to ask.

Immie searched Misha's eyes for a moment, like the words she needed were hidden in Misha's irises. "Right. That *must* be what it feels like to you. Okay. That's a problem that we can't address in just one conversation. It's going to take time. Like I said, for all intents and purposes, I was hired to be your bodyguard, but that was well out of the scope of my normal work. Jeff and I had previously worked on other projects together where I *eliminated* problems, so relationship talks are outside of my wheelhouse. It's like Jeff saw something in me that he thought would work for you on some level. What he didn't think about was that there might be something in you that would complete me. I don't know if that helps, but it's the best way I can think to phrase it."

"You loved me?"

"I love you. To be clear, the fights we've been having weren't an act either. You don't feel like you know where you stand with me, but think about it from my perspective. You're an agent now. You don't need me anymore. The best thing for me to do is to accept that my job here is done and leave as gracefully as I can." It was Immie's turn to get emotional.

"You left me and sent me to be whatever I am now. You wanted to be rid of me." Misha felt the wave of sadness and confusion shift into bitterness.

"No. Absolutely not. I wanted you to refocus. I hated that you lost your job. You're a brilliant woman and an intuitive educator. I thought, hoped, that Jeff might help you find something else, where you could get your shine back. But I've learned that he and I had different ideas on how to do that."

"To be fair, I think he felt a little mixed about doing it. Tell me, why didn't you want me to be an agent?"

"Misha, agents lie, manipulate, abuse, and hold objectives over all else. Sure, you could do that, but that's not who you are when you're at your best. You're one of the few people I know who shines when you aren't hiding anything. You *love* people, and you aren't a rule follower. I don't want to see those parts of you go away, and there's a good chance they would… will if you're going to stay a spy."

"You're right, Immie. I do all of those things now. Maybe I always did." *What was going on here? Misha, you're blowing it by turning everything into blame.* Misha couldn't help it though: she hadn't allowed herself time to pick all of the pieces apart. Now Misha had what she wanted for so long, an opportunity to really talk with Immie again, but the conversation had so much riding on its success that all of the emotions were pouring out of Misha. She couldn't control herself.

"I hear that you're angry. I am too. Like I said, I don't know what to do other than for us to go our separate ways, Mish." Immie looked out the window. It hurt to say this aloud, but it felt like the only option. She turned back and stared Misha in the eye. "I've always loved you. For what it's worth now, that's always been true."

"What does any of this even matter? Immie, you saw those files. People are trying to kill me, and these are people who are really good at killing." Misha couldn't disguise her anger and resentment. "You're right. Your mission is over, and you just said you don't want to be with a spy. Can you do me one last favor, and keep the files safe?" Misha moved to stand up.

"Misha, sit down. That's not exactly what I was saying and you know it."

"What do you want me to say, Immie?" Misha's hands were shaking. This conversation was becoming too much for her.

"Let's take one thing at a time. I don't know how to pick through ten years and tell you everything that happened from an operational standpoint. I think we agree that our relationship is too much for either of us to deal with right now. Before we get into a fight and say more things we can't take back, let's focus on something we *can* handle."

Misha didn't know exactly what Immie meant, but she could agree that this wasn't going the way she'd hoped. "What can we handle?"

"I'm good at wet work, and I understand that you have some abilities as a spy. We should be able to figure out how to keep you alive—if we work together. Let's start there." Immie hoped this attempt at levity would de-escalate the tension of the conversation. Immie couldn't help hearing her own words echo in her head: she did love Misha. There was no harm in trying to pick something small and move from there. Maybe if they had a success, that could be a new starting point for them and if they failed Misha would be dead and it wouldn't matter anyway.

"Okay." Misha accepted Immie's pivot. "The files. I'm in a difficult position, but with your help, I think we might be able to overcome the abysmal odds."

"I know we can, Misha. Once you're safe, then we'll see where we're at. Right now, we'll take baby steps. Talk me through everything you *know*."

Just like that, Misha felt all the crushing emotions dissipate. Immie made it safe for Misha to put all the big relationship stuff on hold while they figured out this life or death problem. It wasn't everything she wanted, but it was a start. So she took the relational armistice and told Immie anything she thought was relevant to the situation and survival. Misha felt good trusting someone and not holding anything back. Immie really listened to her and asked questions as Misha went through her operations in relation to Jeff, Max, and Trevor. She even told Immie the unedited version of Mr. X. Misha decided the risk was worth it because the stakes were high, and she needed to believe someone would know her and still want to see her survive.

CHAPTER 19

TWENTY MID-CAREER EX-SPECIAL FORCES MEN walked into the abandoned warehouse. It was typical as far as empty warehouses go, with broken windows and simplistic graffiti tags on concrete walls. There was also assorted trash in every corner, left behind by rodents, naughty kids, long-gone businesses, and the occasional homeless encampment.

Toward the middle of the room were fifteen student chairs set up in rows, facing a green chalkboard. The ex-special forces men had been told there'd be a debrief, but they hadn't expected this weird scenario. Still, they stood near the faux classroom. They'd followed the instructions they'd been texted: weapons and cell phones were left in the lock boxes outside.

They milled around waiting until they heard the rusty groan of the door on the west side of the building, revealing their newest boss. The older woman walked in purposefully, dressed in a business suit that appeared to be made from upholstery fabric. Her black heels clicked on the concrete floor as she walked to the chalkboard. Standing like an angry schoolteacher, she nodded towards the chairs, which were hardly big enough to hold an elementary school child, let alone 210 pounds of muscle.

A few of the men looked at the chairs and then back at their boss. But she pursed her lips and waited them out until all but five sat down, looking like outtakes from *Kindergarten Cop*. The remaining men stood at the back.

Once everyone was settled, Carol asked, "What did I tell you about the mission?"

One man, scrunched in a chair, raised his hand, and Carol pointed at him. "To secure the owner of HMH Tobacconist and bring him to his location."

"Correct," she replied, before looking around theatrically. "And is he here today?"

"No," a soldier from the back responded. "We had him surrounded. He disappeared somehow."

A man in the front row added, "The official report noted no human remains. Several unregistered weapons and accelerants were at the scene."

Carol's tone became more shrill and condescending. "What did I tell you about this particular mission?"

"You told us to go in quiet and quick, ma'am. We did. You said the codger was a slippery one. We followed all of the best methods for a live capture, but we didn't have enough intel to be effective," a man in the back row said. He stood up and prepared to tell Carol off. But within a second, he collapsed on the floor, with a spring of blood emerging from his head.

The man next to him jumped up in surprise and landed in the same position. The thirteen men still seated scanned the room to find the source. Were the chairs on some sort of mine, or was there a sniper?

"Calm down, gentlemen. Nothing will happen to you as long as you stay where you are. I'm merely illustrating what happens when you go clomping around. When you rush a scene, it sets off every single warning device in a person's arsenal. You're lucky to be alive, given Max's more traditional way of dealing with interlopers. I'm very disappointed in your performance. I expected more than a smash-and-grab approach from twenty highly trained agents like yourselves."

One of the men responded in a voice that sounded like he was trying to talk Carol out of jumping off a tower. "We cut all comms and the power grid for the surrounding city block."

"Did you now? What did you do in case he had a UPS in his outlet and a secondary power supply?"

A few of the men groaned. Of course, a simple UPS at the office store cost twenty bucks and would scream like a banshee if power was interrupted. It was a simple trick for anyone with suspicions that someone was coming for them.

"You all came highly recommended. I gave you clear instructions, and you disregarded them. If I wanted to play cops and robbers, I would have hired a gang. You all should be ashamed of yourselves." Carol looked over the eighteen men in various stages of coping with their employer's disappointment.

She watched and waited for the situation to sink in. Some of them explored the room with their eyes, others prayed, and a few tried to scheme silently with each other. Three of the men in the front row signaled each other through finger taps that they were going to jump her together. Perhaps they believed there was safety in numbers. This futile plan amused Carol, and she took a step closer to them. They couldn't resist the bait and leaped toward her but landed not more than a foot from their chairs, more red spreading on the floor, creating little sticky puddles.

Carol scoffed, "I'm using the very best of drone technology in this room. At this point, I should mention that I only need five of you for the next mission. You lucky five will do the task for free to make up for costing me the man I needed. However, I won't be forgiving if you fail me twice."

A man in the middle row raised his voice. "You say you prepared us well. You told us he was sneaky, not that he was paranoid. You told us he runs a shop, not that he's someone who hides for a living." He held her with his eyes.

"You are correct."

"Why would you withhold information if you wanted the job done right?"

"Why? That's a good question, and if you make it out of here, I might tell you."

"My name is Anthony, and we *will* meet again." He leaned back in his chair.

"As I said, I need five of you at most." Carol flipped the chalkboard over and removed the sheet of paper covering the back of the board. Pictures, documents, diagrams, maps, and assets outlined in detail the requirements of the next job.

"You cunt. You can't do this to us," one of the men spat out.

"But I *am* doing it, and because of your attitude, whoever lives will have to clean up this mess. Remember, I need five of you to handle the problem outlined on the board, and failure will not be tolerated. When the next mission is completed, to my satisfaction, whoever survives can split the money from the first mission. See, I can be generous too. Good day." Carol then clicked her heels back to the door.

One of the men hurled verbal abuse at her, and he must have let his anger distract him from the need to stay still because as Carol was walking out the door, there was a sudden stop to his taunts and a thud. She smiled and let the door slam behind her. They wouldn't disappoint her again.

CHAPTER 20

FOR THREE DAYS, MISHA AND Immie luxuriated in every pleasure imaginable in the ryokan outside of Kyoto. She'd splurged on a room with soundproofing. This turned out to be a great gift to the neighboring vacationers, as Immie got louder the more relaxed she became, while the lovers reacquainted themselves. They'd found so many new ways to engage each other: feeding each other dinner, walking in the woods, soaking in the public baths looking out at the lake. They talked about things long overdue for discussion. Sometimes their voices would rise with anger or frustration. Other times, they'd fall into giggles. Each excursion and conversation would end the same, sweating and panting in the bed, covered in each other until they lay exhausted. On one occasion, even a private family bath slipped from relaxing calmness into greedy excitement.

It's unlikely that these activities were what the Home Office had in mind when it sent the message "Go to Tokyo immediately. Possible asset. Pose as a tourist."

However, Misha was feeling pleased with her ability to do her job and create cover so expertly. Every time she thought of work, she'd reach out to Immie and start the game all over again. The casual verbal flirting, the looks, the secret touches, and then the love-making like both their lives depended on it.

Misha's favorite was always the evenings, when they'd retire to their room for the night. She saw these as the moments for her to make up with her beautiful wife. She'd start by begging her delicate toes for forgiveness, with the lightest touch of her fingers. She'd move up slowly to the shapely belly to kiss the pain away, lingering over the upturned breasts, kissing and massaging away her mistakes. Then she'd disappear into the deep blue starlight of Immie's eyes, asking questions that started the same every time: "May we now…?" "May we now kiss?", "… forgive each other?", "… be happily in love?", and "… fuck?". And when Immie's eyes answered yes to all of these questions, Misha would feel her and try to soothe all the parts of her body that were hardened with sadness. After driving her to the edge of ecstasy, Misha would keep her there as long as possible, stretching into the abyss of passion.

The morning was Misha's second-favorite time of day, when Immie would wake her with smooth, firm movements of her hand across her back or stomach or butt—a touch that demanded Misha pay attention. As her sleep receded, Misha would rise to meet Immie's firm touch, sighs giving ways to light moans, and finally deep growls from somewhere so far inside that only Immie could reach. And when it was all winding down, Immie would kiss Misha as if the whole world was coming to an end. There had never been kisses like this before. One advantage of healing a rift in a marriage was the balm created by overcoming despair together.

Misha was enjoying her life. Things that hadn't made any sense before were now falling into place.

On the fourth morning, Misha had to forgo the loving touches of her highly imaginative wife and return to Tokyo. She needed to go to the embassy "to request some help with her passport," where she'd find out her actual mission. So the second honeymoon would have to come to an end. Bliss can't last forever. Misha felt herself sighing as the world of simple joys went back to the realities of life: the packing and quiet breakfast, a new hotel in the city, and the uncertainty of what waited at the embassy and after.

It was probably nothing good. Misha wasn't as naïve as she'd been a few months earlier. She remembered that there was at least one person in the world who wanted her dead. But grounded again in her relationship and feeling more confident of who she was at her core gave her strength. She felt the parts of herself coming together. She'd worked through her memories and had integrated the new information. At the end of the introspection, she felt familiar to herself and well prepared to take on her adversary.

Kissing Immie once more before they left the ryokan felt bittersweet for them both. The growth of love where the field had been almost barren was a joy, but the risk to that crop by the push and pull of life seemed overwhelming. They headed out on the train and held hands, determined that their love would be stronger than the challenges ahead of them.

Misha let go of Immie at the hotel and headed to the embassy. She'd decided to make the most of her tourist cover, putting on an ivory boho dress with a small floral pattern. It made her look a bit like an ingénue.

The U.S. embassy, like so many embassies across the globe, was an ugly office building of concrete and darkened windows, a fortress of a building that lent no beauty to the soil it sat upon. At the reception desk, Misha explained to the clerk that she hoped to see Mount Fuji with her girlfriend but had accidentally torn a page in her passport and was worried that someone would ask to see it and decide it had been defaced. The crocodile tears began, and the receptionist ushered Misha down a back corridor and into a tiny room.

After ten minutes, a large man with a bald head, who reminded Misha of Harry Potter's uncle, entered the room. He was looking at some papers in his hand and didn't make eye contact with Misha as he broke into a lecture on how to treat a passport.

"It says here that you've been in Japan for three days, and you damaged your passport two days ago. You absolutely shouldn't have waited this long to come in. I should revoke your passport, and then what will you do? You can't travel until you have a passport, and it could take weeks for a new one to be processed *if* you have the correct paperwork." He looked up from his papers and slowly took in Misha.

Everyone appreciates a solid cover story, but this guy is over the top. "I'm sorry, sir. Does that mean I won't be able to go to Mount Fuji with my girlfriend? Is there anything you can do to help me?"

"I don't know," the man grumbled. "I *shouldn't* help you. You're another young woman with no appreciation for the law or responsibility. Did you think it's okay to come to another country and treat it like it's your living room? You're a guest here, and you should show some respect if you know what that means. Women like you disgust me. I think it might take a *long* time before we can get you the correct passport."

"I'm sorry. It really was an accident. Can't we fix it with tape?" Misha was trying to stay in character, but his performance was beginning to concern her. They were in a secure room alone. He could just tell her what he needed to or pass her a clue as to where a more secure location could be found.

"Tape a passport! *No*, you *can't* tape a passport. It's illegal.

You've broken the law by damaging federal property. I could throw you in jail."

That's when Misha caught it: the passport agent was sweating profusely, and he didn't look at her when he spoke. This man was, in some way, compromised. The role of patriarchal passport clerk might come naturally to him, but he wasn't trying to sell the information exchange—someone had gotten to him first.

"Well, I shouldn't do this, but you seem repentant. You are repentant, aren't you?"

"Of course. I'll do what it takes to make it right." Misha was focused now and hoped to get more information from this man.

"Fine." He handed her a card from the top of the pile of papers. "Come to this address tonight at nine. I'll see what I can do to help you."

"Thank you so much. Is this a second embassy?"

"Just be there," he said, as he left the room.

She rushed to the hotel and found Immie half-dressed, dancing to music in the bathroom while putting on her make-up.

"Hey… so, they're going to try to kill me," Misha said calmly.

Immie turned to kiss Misha. "I prefer my lovers warm, intact, and alive."

"You're so picky." Misha leaned against the doorframe. "We'll need to come up with a plan, as I have a meeting at nine p.m. at an address listed on an embassy business card." Misha started to write "embassy" with her fingertip on the bathroom counter.

"Alright." Immie quickly finished her make-up, took the card from Immie, and went back into the bedroom. She opened her laptop, and Misha watched as she located the address on Google maps. "Google has the best free spyware around. Let's learn about this place."

"It's in Shibuya, Immie, so there won't be anything special about it. My guess is it's where they'll take my phone before ushering me to a second location, where I'll disappear forever. Maybe my body will end up in Roppongi, or maybe I'll vanish."

"Hmm… perhaps I should go with you?" Immie smiled.

Misha felt calmer than she thought she should be, but then again, this was the first time she trusted anyone she worked with at all. "Thanks, but I'm sure they have a contingency plan if I come with backup. I think you'll need to lend a hand from a safe distance."

"Perhaps we can get a message to Jeff?"

"I don't think he could help. He's good at getting me *into* situations but ill-equipped to get me out of them." Misha started to bite her lower lip. "Hmm… what about Trevor? But, no, I can't do that either to protect his anonymity. My protocols for making contact won't work with low-security hotel Wi-Fi."

"Losers don't get laid, so you'll have to think of something," Immie said, repeating the tease she used when they'd play one-on-one soccer in the park.

Misha accepted that Immie couldn't come with her to the meeting, but that didn't mean she couldn't be part of the plan. "Immie, do you have any connections around here?"

"Maybe, but I'd have to head out and see who's around." Immie's eyes already seemed to be searching the streets of Japan, finding dangerous people she could trust with this kind of mission. "We'd need a tight team that can handle assassins, and they couldn't be CIA-affiliated."

"Agreed." Misha loved to watch Immie think through a plan. Her knowledge about the cosmos was equal to her ability to see a problem coming from a mile away.

"Okay." Immie got up, grabbed her bag, and left. When she had a goal, she was unstoppable. Once Misha had interrupted her when she was trying to finish the last page of a paper on black holes. The interruption led to three additional days of writing and one grumpy Immie.

But now on her own in the room, Misha could feel the fear rising up inside her again. After two failed attempts, she presumed this next assassin or assassin team would have a long, successful history. She didn't want to run and hide, but nor did she want to live with a target on her back. With Immie by her side again, Misha felt the hope of a new life, where there was room for them both to grow, individually and together. She knew she needed to survive, and get information from her would be assassins, if she hoped to have the future she deserved with Immie.

Misha entered Casa de Amigo restaurant, close to Shibuya Station. It was a delightful surprise to see Mexican food in Japan. Forgetting everything else for a moment, she sat down at the counter and studied the menu. There was nothing like finding the food you love from home when traveling abroad. Misha had been complaining about the food to Immie, saying it was the thing that made her most homesick. She ordered chips with salsa, and a margarita, imagining how great the drink of lime-sweetened goodness would taste. Then she was interrupted from her reverie by someone standing too close behind her.

Without turning around, Misha knew it was the man from the embassy. He smelled like bureaucracy—molding papers in dusty Manila folders. "We need to leave now," he said.

"But Uncle Jake, I've just ordered. It will be here in a minute. Let's talk. The first cerveza is on me," Misha said at top American volume.

"Uncle Jake" scanned the crowded bar and sat at the barstool to her right. Misha came to two conclusions from his haste to comply with her order. First, he didn't have a full plan, and he certainly hadn't planned for contingencies. Second, he had no control in this situation, so there must be someone else. Time to work the puppet over and see who was pulling the strings.

"A cerveza for my uncle," Misha said to the bartender before turning to face this cowardly man with his weak intimidation strategies. "So, what's the play here?"

"I don't have to tell you anything. Pay for the food, take a few bites, and then we need to leave." He was sweating, the nervous kind of sweat that smelled a little like vomit. He really was disgusting.

"Alternatively," Misha said, "you could leave your phone here and go. I'm guessing this isn't your scene, so let's end our acquaintance here, and I'll deal with whoever sent you to collect me." She was making a small leap, seeing what she could learn from a confident guess.

"I can't. I'm not supposed to leave your side until we get to the destination."

Bingo. Shot in the dark for the win. This guy was stuck in a pot. Based on his intimidation style and penchant for misogynistic comments, it had to be a full-on honey pot. The bastard must have taken liberties with women in the past. Gross. What kind of information would he even have?

"How are you supposed to communicate with our friend?"

"I don't. He'll meet us." Now Uncle was visibly sweating everywhere.

"I can see you're scared. You can wait here in the restaurant and leave later. There's no reason for you to be involved anymore. Where's the meeting place?"

"I have to go with you."

"Any other instructions?"

"No... I don't want to do this."

The food and drinks were placed on the counter. Misha shared the chips and salsa, but the embassy man ate so slowly that it was clearly an effort for him. Given his fear and lack of knowledge, he must be aware that it might be the last thing he'd ever eat.

"Okay. We'll do this together. Tell me where we're going."

"I just said I can't tell you."

"Tell me where we're going, or I'll leave you here and walk away."

He winced. "If you don't go where they told me to take you, they'll kill us." He started crying softly to himself, like he was a mourner at his own funeral.

"Well, Mr. Brightside, it sounds like we're going for a walk. People have tried to kill me before, so it doesn't bother me much. But I can see you don't want to try it, so, for the last time, tell me where you're taking me."

"Shinagawa Station, by the harbor."

Misha took a chug of her margarita with one hand while disengaging the phone in her jacket with the other. "Time to go, Uncle."

On the way to the station, the embassy man had a hard time keeping up with Misha, whose developing philosophy was to run at danger and hope it flinched first. At the station, he tried to buy tickets from a machine but was shaking so much that he gave up and bought them from the station agent instead.

As they boarded the train for Shinagawa, Misha scanned the cabin suspiciously. There were kids out for the night toward the front and one tired-looking man in a suit a few rows behind them. Nothing was out of the ordinary.

Stop after stop, there was a lot of regular activity, but no-one tried to get close to her or her embassy escort. When they finally got off, the night air was chilly due to the proximity to the sea. Misha positioned herself near possible barriers and in lighting that wasn't optimal for snipers, doing everything she learned at the CIA camp. The man from the embassy looked baffled and started to speak when a gorilla of a man stepped out of the shadows behind him. Then Uncle Jake was silent. The man half-dragged him a few feet away onto a bench and left him slumped over. He wouldn't be bothering pretty girls who came to the embassy anymore.

Misha waited in the shadow of the building, taking in all the information she could about this man. He had the typical muscular CIA look, and his movements were judicious and rhythmic.

"Come with me," he said, in a demanding tone without anger, typical of someone used to people doing as he said.

"No, thanks." Misha was curious about what would happen when Goliath didn't get his way.

"It wasn't a request. You need to come with me now."

"But you've just killed the man who brought me here, and I have the whole stranger-danger vibe. I know I should never go anywhere with strangers, especially when they don't even offer candy so, as I said, no thanks." This level of snark was the only way Misha could push back without showing her concern about how to neutralize a man at least twice her size and quadruple her strength. Cocky made her feel in control. It was only a small thing, but it lent her a lot of power.

The huge man pulled back his jacket, revealing a Glock 22 S&W. Misha's mind began to process the gun and what it could mean here in Japan, along with the way he used the knife on Uncle on the bench. Goliath wasn't CIA. Probably private military—a fucking contractor. Misha figured he was likely KBR, but maybe MVM or Academi. That type of soldier no longer had a little voice in the back of their head telling them violence against other humans was wrong: it had been waterboarded from years of seeing shit that couldn't be unseen and now stared blankly out of the frontal lobe. Goliath was precisely who you'd send when you wanted to recover some lost documents and disappear a problematic agent. There was no way a conversation was possible. She had minutes, though more likely seconds, before this situation would become unsurvivable for her.

"Look, man, I'm here for the same reason you are: to see if we can create an asset. So why don't we sit down and talk through the plan?" It was a weak move, but Misha felt it worked better than pissing herself and kicking him in the shins, most likely in that order, damn margarita.

"We'll leave now." He turned around and started walking.

Misha knew she had to follow, but she kept five feet behind, scanning for options. But seeing no simple way out and not wanting to disappear from the train station, she shouted in his general direction, "My safe word is 'papaya!'" If she hadn't been so scared, she would have laughed. The papaya phrase was an Immie addition for calling in help. Of course, Immie would make Misha shout that out something ridiculous at a deserted metro station.

As Goliath turned around to face Misha, another man came up next to him. Goliath punched him, but on the other side was another man, who plunged a syringe in his neck. And, as the Bible will tell you, Goliath went down.

A news van pulled up. The two men dragged Goliath inside, and Misha hopped in the back. They took off into the night. After driving through streets and side streets for longer than Misha cared to spend in a confined space with the now unarmed man (she held onto his gun), the van eventually stopped. They'd pulled up in front of a tan brick building with a white street-level garage and a brown door leading into an alleyway. The sound of bass from a nearby nightclub was banging out the doors and down the street. Misha jumped out of the truck. The men carried the massive body of the mercenary between them like a passed-out drunk to the door, which Immie was holding open. They followed Immie inside and downstairs to an underground apartment.

Immie guided the men through a small living area, taking Goliath into a partially soundproofed bedroom. Unfortunately, the dose of tranquilizer injected into him had obviously not been enough because he suddenly flung the man on his left against the wall and punched the man on his right. Both would have been left immobilized, except Goliath was still groggy. He lunged for the chair but missed it and then straightened up and set Misha in his sights. Misha took one step back and pulled the Glock out of her waistband. But Goliath wasn't going to stop over a little thing like a gun pointed at his solar plexus—he had a mission to complete, or die trying. He took one running step toward Misha before Immie kicked him in the side of the knee. He stumbled to the ground. The two men were up again and struggled to corner him, but they didn't have control of the situation. Immie moved nimbly, dodging him, and landing punches that connected cleanly with his face. She and the two men secured Goliath to a chair and gave him another shot of something.

Once Goliath was fully secured, Immie nodded, and the guys from the van left. Immie talked to Goliath in a voice so icy that Misha felt the chill in her spine. She'd never seen Immie like this before, not even during their worst fights.

"What were you going to do to Agent Campbell?" Immie reached down and removed Goliath's leather belt. She wrapped it around her hand, leaving a few inches and the buckle hanging. She whipped it across Goliath's cheek, causing a big gash. "I see you brought a gun. Who else is with you?"

Silence.

She evened out his cheeks. His face was bleeding and blooming into large welt-raised bruises. If she did this much more, he soon wouldn't be recognizable.

Misha returned the gun to her waistband and watched as Immie continued to lash Goliath with the belt buckle, spreading the pain across the most sensitive parts of his body. Although he was panting and blood was seeping through his clothes, he still said nothing. Before each hit, Immie asked a question, sometimes repeating previous questions, sometimes asking simple questions. At other times, she asked things so complex that Misha couldn't follow them.

After forty-five minutes, Goliath started providing one-word answers. After an hour, he was giving up information that may or may not be reliable. After an hour and a half, Immie opened the door and walked out.

As Misha followed, Goliath made another noise, causing her to turn around. Against her better judgment, she went over to him and knelt down. She couldn't be sure, but it sounded as if he said "Max."

"What about Max?"

Goliath kept repeating the word, but he didn't, or couldn't, acknowledge Misha. She gave up and went to the next room to find Immie.

When Immie saw Misha enter the living room, she said, "He isn't worth any more to me, one way or the other." The battered men from the van stood up and headed back into the bedroom.

Misha's mind was reeling with the relief of surviving again. The information Goliath provided was unlikely to be actionable, as it was given after a lot of duress. Misha hadn't looked around the living area of the apartment as they headed into the bedroom with Goliath. Now her eyes scanned the room and noticed a new person, a waif-like platinum blonde dressed head to toe in black. She looked like a stylist from a high-end salon, and massively out of place in this basement apartment turned interrogation center.

"Misha, this is Miranda," Immie said as she walked over and put the kettle on a small stovetop.

"Misha," said Miranda, "find something to change into

from the suitcase and leave everything you wore here in a pile. Everything." Miranda nodded toward a carry-on in the corner of the room.

Immie stripped off her blood-splattered clothing and headed naked into the bathroom with a kitchen towel, to get the residue of Goliath off her skin. Misha rummaged through the suitcase. She settled on black and white high-waist palazzo pants, a supportive chemise, yellow silk blouse, and black ballet flats. As she was changing, she heard the faint but distinct sound of power tools. When Immie returned from the bathroom, she added the bloodied towel to the discarded clothes and grabbed a black jumpsuit from the suitcase.

"Sit, please," said Miranda to Misha. "We must hurry." Miranda began to fix Misha's hair, adding spray color.

Immie chatted with Miranda. If a pile of bloody clothes and a gun weren't on the floor, it would be like they were having a fun ladies' night in. After Miranda finished applying make-up to Misha, Immie gave Misha a cup of tea and took her place in the chair.

After a while, Miranda paused her ministrations to check her phone. "Okay, we've got ten minutes. Neither of you has anything on you—guns, GPS, identifying documents—correct?" Immie and Misha both nodded, and Misha added, "I put his gun over there."

"No problem. We can get rid of that." Miranda returned to Immie's make-up.

When Misha and Immie were ready, Miranda opened the door and checked there was no-one in the stairway. She led them back up the stairway, and instead of going the way they came it, they went left down the thin exterior corridor to an entry in the wall that opened into the back of the nightclub. Immie took

Misha's hand and whispered in her ear, "You look unbelievably beautiful. We're two socialites heading out to our waiting car."

As they worked their way slowly between tables filled with the young and vibrant, Immie embraced people warmly like they were dear friends and danced and laughed. Misha was in awe of how talented Immie was at blending in to the setting. When they eventually emerged from the pounding musical paradise onto the street, a town car was waiting for them.

"Harold, to the jet," Immie said to the man holding the door open.

CHAPTER 21

SITING AT THE MOST BORING dinner party in existence, Jeff Martin was trying to discreetly exchange filthy text messages with his younger lover, who was currently in Mykonos, high on ecstasy. Jeff was feeling very jealous. He listened to a diplomat drone on about the need to protect an oil company from "the natives." Like it was the 1800s in a British men's club. Fuckers. This was the type of meeting Jeff hated having to attend, listen to and report back on, as if the ways of rich robber barons ever changed.

Peering down at his phone again and seeing the image of a sizeable erection was enough of a reason to excuse himself from the table. "I'm sorry," he said. "This text won't wait. I need to handle it right now."

Heading off to the guest bathroom, he was hopeful that the dinner might be an enjoyable occasion after all. On the way, he faked a call in the hallway. The texts were coming in rapid fire now.

In the quaint Laura Ashley rose-wallpapered bathroom were boxes of tissues and a lovely rose-smelling lotion. It was like they *wanted* people to masturbate in here. The texts and pictures popping up on his phone were becoming filthier by the second—photos of his boyfriend with different people, and videos of beautiful people passionately entwined. Jeff was so hard now that he could barely contain himself. Standing in front of the mirror, he dropped his pants slightly and applied the rose lotion. Then, with his cock in one hand and cell phone in the other, he kept watching the pictures coming through, remembering all the times he'd been in that situation with his boyfriend. He was getting so close. But the next text was from Misha. He hurried to slide it away. She texted him again. Ugh. There was nothing she could be texting him that couldn't wait two minutes.

Jeff went back to the live stream from his boyfriend and his night of debauchery. It was essential to clear one's head before attempting important work. But no sooner had Jeff taken in an image of his boyfriend with a man and a woman, the texts from Misha began again. He gave up on his erection, feeling his balls grow a bit heavier and his attitude becoming significantly more cranky.

Breathing deeply, he attempted to sort out what Misha was requesting of him. He knew he'd have to leave the party and call her, but at least she'd given him an excuse to leave this abysmal dinner. First, though, he had to text his lover to tell him to stop sharing for the time being. Hopefully, things with Misha would be easy to fix, and he could catch up with him a little later.

As Jeff drove home, there wasn't a single text from Misha. It was like her problem got magically better when he left the party. The lights were on in his house. He parked and slowly reached under his seat and pulled out his gun holstered there. It was an inconvenient time to have to deal with a home invasion, but needs must. However, as he quietly entered through the back door, he could hear Misha's laughter coming from the kitchen. This might be the worst part of having his best friend become a spy: she was more annoying than ever before. Jeff began to prepare a lecture on how you can't just blow up someone's phone and then break into their house. As he came around the corner, he saw not just Misha but Immie too, sitting at his bar. This was worse than being stuck with onerous diplomats. Misha and Immie had broken into his house. This could not be good.

"You didn't tell me you were bringing a friend."

Immie bounded over and kissed Jeff on the cheek with mock enthusiasm. "Oh, Jeffery, I've missed you too."

"Where's the oddest place you've ever masturbated, Jeff?" Misha said as she stood up to hug him too.

"What?"

"She means have you ever masturbated anywhere stranger than that rose-covered bathroom?" Immie started giggling.

"*What?*" Jeff repeated.

"I've learned a few things about surveillance since school, Teach." Misha giggled too. "We need to talk." She poured a cup of tea for each of them.

"It sounds like you've learned more than enough." He didn't like how they were being jovial and trying to put him on guard at the same time.

"I need to know what you know about all of it: me, the program, Max." Misha looked at him seriously now.

"Looks like my baby girl is all grown up. This is what you pulled me home for? We could have discussed this tomorrow, without the added surveillance." Jeff was giving Misha side-eye as he sipped his tea.

"Pulling you out of the party was fun, and coitus interruptus sounds like a spell you need more of in your life." Immie giggled again as she let the steam furl around her heart-shaped face.

"Okay, what do you want to know?"

"Everything."

"Well, I know you're a fantastic lay, and that you drive men to write ridiculous books in the forlorn hope of winning you back by destroying your career." If Misha wanted something specific, she could come out and ask it. In the last few months, she'd been a wild card. He never knew what she was thinking or where she was going. At first, he'd given her space so she could find her way with so much new information. And more recently, she wanted a purely professional relationship, and even though it hurt, he respected her wishes. But showing up like this was just distasteful, so he decided a barbed response was warranted.

"That's low," Misha retorted.

"Oh, I forgot something: and you spy on your best friend while he's at work. So you're a dubious character, at best."

"Dick." Misha looked down at the counter and started tracing the word "dick" in various sized letters with her finger. Why was he being like this?

"Be more specific. I can't read your mind," he said.

"What else do you know?" Misha didn't want to guide him too much.

"What do you mean, 'What else'? That's it. I told you everything I knew months ago." Jeff was no clearer as to why Misha wanted him here right now. "Did you call me here to what... officiate your renewal of vows?"

"We're back together. You're right." Immie gave an exaggerated grin, knowing it would irritate Jeff.

He glared at her. "*Mazel tov.*"

"What about the program and Max?" Misha hoped to shake something loose in Jeff's memories.

"You met Max. What did he tell you about the program? It's not my program. *You* were my assignment."

"You don't know anything else?" Misha found it hard to believe that Jeff didn't have more information.

"Max doesn't like to cross-pollenate. He tells me what I need to know when I need to know it. Max is my boss, Misha. He told me I needed to become your best friend. I did, and we are. He told me I was in charge of keeping you safe, so I found you a few girlfriends and boyfriends." He paused to relish the flinch in Immie, then continued with a smirk, "Immie refused to resign from the job. That's all I know about the program: my part. My only directive is to keep you safe, and so far, I'm doing great. But if you want more from me, you have to be specific, and if you want intel, you're certainly barking up the wrong tree." Jeff surprised himself with how direct he was being. Maybe it was the desire to get back to his phone, or perhaps it was time to move forward. The more he and Misha had to work together, the more closed off from him she'd become. He didn't know if the change in their relationship had cost him his best friend. Right now, he figured it was easier to burn it all down.

"Are you telling the truth?" The question was on the nose, but Misha couldn't think of a better way to ask for this information.

"Of course I am. Why would I start lying to you now?"

Immie looked up at both of them and then nodded to Misha. She saw that Immie was confirming her assessment.

"You can't help me? I thought you had all this power. You aren't Max's right-hand man, are you?" Misha sunk on her barstool. It was time to think of a new tactic.

"Sweetie, I'm a competent and powerful-ish man. I have my piece of the pie, and it's lucrative, easy, and relatively safe. I don't want more trouble than I can handle. So why don't you tell me specifically what you're looking for, and we can see if I can help you find it? That's where I excel: finding things." Jeff smiled at her. She wasn't trying to push him away. She was just being her usual self-absorbed self and not considering how she was coming across.

"Okay. Why did you send me to Japan?" Misha realized she'd have to lead him down the rabbit hole to find out why he sold her out. It was impossible to believe he didn't know more about something. If information was his thing, maybe he needed to be asked directly why so many of her missions resulted in assassination attempts.

"When did you go to Japan? I'm your handler, and I haven't sent you anywhere." Jeff stared at Misha.

"Yes, you did, via emails, as always."

"I most certainly did *not* send you to Japan. As far as I knew, you were back in California spending time with Immie."

"They tried to kill me in Japan. It's the third time, and the only person who sends me anywhere is supposed to be you. So what are you and Max up to that I'm walking around with a target on my back? Did you decide it was easier for the program to eradicate the outed agent?" Misha studied Jeff's face, trying to gauge his reaction.

Jeff looked at Misha, carefully weighing the truth about the situation. Immie's presence now was making a great deal of sense: Misha had brought herself an interrogator. So Jeff needed to measure his words, because he wasn't interested in merely surviving, but in walking through the flame unscathed. He hadn't done anything wrong, and he wasn't going to take the blame for whatever this was.

"Mish, I think there's a lot you're not telling me. As I said, we're friends, and as far as a working relationship goes, my job is to keep you alive. Please start filling me in on what's going on with you so that I can do my job. I need to know about all three times in detail. Think about that for a second. I'll be right back." Jeff walked to the drawer in the kitchen and pulled out a pen, a pad of paper, and a small machine that he plugged into the wall and made strange metallic sounds.

He sat down again and nodded towards the machine. "That's the new transmitter blocker. It should give us additional protection if there are any bugs in the room. But your cell phones will be shit right now. Okay. Please take your time, spare no detail, and presume I know nothing, which is feeling like the case."

Misha thought this was strange. She'd never had Jeff's undivided attention before. "Why should I tell you shit? You need to tell me about Max."

"Well then, we're at an impasse because I have no information for you. It does seem like you've gone pretty far off book without checking in with me. Max and I told you everything I knew after Budapest. That was when we confirmed that you were a target. Unless you're going to talk to me, I can't help you with information or resources. It seems that you're the one holding back a lot of information here. So let me catch up, or you can ransack my house, torture me, and still never know more. Are we friends or not?" Jeff hated being in this position.

"Paris… they… they killed Mr. X."

"No, they didn't. He filed from Singapore last week." Jeff couldn't understand what Misha was saying—Mr. X had been very helpful in some complex economic deals.

"I saw his brains come out of his head in a Paris hotel room. So your intel is incorrect."

"Shit. Okay. We have some work to do. Tell me about Paris, because after that agent disappeared, I got you on a plane and home safely. So I think you might have left out the part about being in a hotel room with an agent that had already burned you once."

Neither Misha nor Jeff fully trusted each other, but both of their statements and responses left enough space for miscommunication and mishaps that they were ready to negotiate through information gently. For the next two hours, they went round for round, looking at the problems and information under Immie's watchful eye.

They discussed and deliberated about Mr. X, Trevor, the files from First Democrats PAC, and the fire that destroyed Max's shop. Periodically, Immie would add a detail or ask a question to make sure the two heard each other fully. Jeff and Immie had never had a good relationship. They'd fought over operational details on every mission they'd ever run together. But both of them respected the role the other played in Misha's life. As the conversation progressed, the three started to develop a cohesiveness that none of them had ever anticipated.

Misha finished with, "I came here tonight because I know I can't run. I came here to see if you could help, or if you are an obstacle. I believe now you can help."

Jeff pushed his notepad aside and looked at the counter where Misha periodically spelled out their conversation. He rubbed his temples, thinking about everything Misha had told him and trying to ignore the feeling of dread about what they were up against. "I wish Max was here. He must have figured out who your adversary is, which would explain his absence—someone forced him to go into hiding. But the three of us have something better: we know you. That's more than enough to make a powerful offensive attack."

"I told you he's not as dumb as he looks," Immie said with a twinkle in her eye. She pulled a sheet of paper out of her back pocket and placed it in front of Jeff.

The sheet had four names on it. Jeff studied the names, then studied Immie and Misha.

"We believe at least one of these four people is a member of the Boardroom," said Misha. "We need you to use your tools and connections to figure out which one or ones we need to move our plan forward. Then we're going to quickly and quietly bring this organization to a halt." Misha put her hand on Jeff's. "And that should be enough to protect me and the others."

"I'm familiar with all of them, but they're nobodies. They don't have enough power to lobby McDonald's to make a Big Mac. Apart from General Hanover, and he is all but retired."

"I know it seems that way. But trust me: one of these people is vital to us achieving our goal. We need an in. Immie has all the background and will walk you through it, but I need to do something else tonight." Misha didn't say any more, for what would she say? Her hope of finding her adversary lay in putting pressure on one of the four men, based on guesses from going through a handful of documents. But at least it was a plan. Now she needed to see if she could hedge their bet.

CHAPTER 22

"WHAT IS THIS?" SAID CAROL in her sharp schoolteacher voice. She was on the partially constructed tenth floor of a new building on Capitol One Boulevard, staring at three of the five men who'd failed her, again, and one battered woman hogtied on the floor.

"Its name is Miranda," the speaker for the group said. "Miranda killed Bill."

"Who's Bill?" Carol looked at the tattletale, a giant beefcake of a man with the maturity of a ten-year-old. She decided it would be better when he was dead.

"One of our team. The survivors from… um… the other thing. That warehouse thing," Beefcake replied.

"So, you failed." Carol tried to contain her fury at this level of incompetence.

Beefcake and the henchmen exchanged a look. "She knew we were coming for her. Someone tipped her off. That's how Jim got killed. That bitch kidnapped and killed Jim!" Beefcake looked to Carol for some compassion over the fall of Bill and Jim. Carol tried to remember what they looked like, only to recall she didn't care.

"I'd ask your name, but there's no point in remembering it.

You, Bill, Jim, and these two failed me twice. I appreciate you grouping yourselves to make killing you easier."

"No, ma'am. We brought you Miranda, and she can tell you everything you need to know about some agent safeguarding your target. You didn't tell us that this agent has a full protection detail. Our assassination plans didn't include a contingency plan for the agent being a protected person. Take Miranda and leave. We can't work with you when you aren't communicative about the conditions." At this statement, the henchmen sat up a little straighter and pulled out guns, which they all aimed at Carol.

"Until a month ago, you were working as contractors for the U.S. military overseas. Contingency planning is supposed to be your strong suit. I will not apologize for your incompetence." Carol waited and watched the men. One was starting to scratch his throat absentmindedly. It would be a two-minute conversation, based on her calculations. She figured she'd need to improvise for a few moments more. "Why didn't you learn anything from our last conversation? I didn't send you to kill innocents. I've sent you twice to kill operators. I gave you notes, instructions, and motivation. I cannot account for arrogance or poor planning. I'm afraid you're correct about one thing: I won't need any of you any longer."

The henchmen's coughing was too distracting for Carol to bother continue talking. Instead, she leaned back against the doorway and observed the two men fall from their chairs, clutching at their throats and convulsing. Their bodies became still, as greenish foam and liquid trickled out of their slack mouths.

Beefcake stared at them as if he'd never seen anyone die before. Watching people you know personally die was much more intimate than killing people from a distance. That was the most significant difference Carol had noticed with the younger generations: they play so many video games that they've forgotten there were real consequences to any action taken. She'd seen things that would make these men shit their pants, or rather would make Beefcake shit his pants. The others had already done this.

"Now, Beefcake, I'm probably going to kill you soon. I don't want to get your hopes up for a happy ending that isn't coming. However, there's a small chance you might impress me. If that happens, we'll negotiate."

"If you're talking to me, my name is Anthony." He took a step closer to his fallen brothers-in-arms and in the process tripped over Miranda. When he righted himself, he came up with his gun pointing at Carol.

"Put that away, Beefcake. You don't have a prayer at getting a single round out of the barrel. Think about what you know about me already." She waited patiently, like a teacher who's asked a pupil for an answer that she knows will take him a while to figure out. Finding Beefcake short of the ability to follow simple orders or do long division in his head, she tried a different tactic. "Tell me what you learned from Miranda here."

Miranda had been silent up to this point, squeezing her eyes shut and trying to squirm away from the dead men. Now she looked at Carol and sighed, resigned to her fate in precisely the opposite way of Anthony. Miranda could do the mental math, and she knew that her chance of survival here was nearly zero.

"Well, she's an old associate of a woman who goes by the name Immie. They've been on missions together on and off for over fifteen years. Immie is exceptionally skilled and dangerous. According to Miranda, her team was hired the day we were supposed to apprehend the target, and we missed her by minutes."

"Okay, I'd like to hear from Miranda now." Carol's voice had picked up its sharp edge again. "Miranda, how loyal are you to this Immie?"

Anthony removed the gag, and Miranda spit. "My loyalty is purchased, not earned."

Carol shot Anthony in the head without even looking in his direction, and he went down like a felled tree. "Very well. I require a mercenary who can track down two agents and kill them for me. I believe you're familiar with the targets and the risks involved."

Miranda raised her bound wrists in front of her as best she could in response. Carol fished around in her pocket and then tossed a Swiss Army knife in her general direction. As she was leaving, she said, "Bring them both to the address I send you. I'll text it to Beefcake's phone."

As Carol took the elevator down, she felt relieved to be working with someone who understood the job. Miranda didn't call out or ask any stupid questions. Carol didn't even feel the need to tell her to clean up: she'd figure that out for herself. If this new one could deliver, Carol might consider bringing her into the Boardroom. She seemed easy enough to motivate, and the Boardroom was in dire need of more women. Maybe Miranda could be the new McDougal's replacement. Carol didn't care for his accent. Maybe it was time to let go of Joshua. He was such a presuming ass—Carol hated gin. But it was important to see if Miranda could deliver first.

CHAPTER 23

MISHA HAD BEEN IN MANY homes and offices without an invitation. She'd placed bugs and gone through people's personal effects, looking for information that would inspire someone to become an asset. However, walking without permission into the home of someone she'd known intimately was a new experience.

Misha hadn't seen Ryan in over fifteen years, but it was like no time had passed. She entered through the kitchen door in the back of the house. She slid the lockpick set back into her pocket and pulled out a flashlight. In the kitchen, she saw a wooden spatula hanging from a little piece of rawhide on the wall next to the stove. It was Ryan's grandmother's special chili spoon: her lucky charm that she credited for winning the county chili challenge five years in a row. She gave the spoon and the recipe to Ryan when he graduated from college. When he told Misha this, his eyes had sparkled. That man loved his grandma… and chili. Misha touched the spoon and smiled, thinking of his happiness. However, the information she needed was unlikely to be in the kitchen, so she walked to the hallway.

In the hallway, she noted that there were no pictures on the wall other than Ryan's family, and no signs that he was cohabitating with a roommate or an intimate partner. It was like he'd stopped acquiring personal objects twenty years before, which filled Misha's chest with sadness.

Standing in the doorway, she scanned the room. The illumination from the street lights was enough for her to see the basic details. On one wall was a *Reservoir Dogs* poster. Underneath this was Ryan's grandfather's wingback leather chair. Opposite the chair was the flag that had been draped over his uncle's casket, now lovingly folded and displayed in a triangular box. Everywhere Misha looked, there were reminders of Ryan's family. Even the bouquet Misha caught at his cousin's wedding. Aside from the movie poster, there was nothing to suggest who Ryan was other than a tribute to his family. That was Misha's problem when they dated: she never felt certain who Ryan was. They hadn't dated long, but she was sure that to stay with him would mean becoming an object, a statue of the woman he put on a pedestal. It made her feel claustrophobic.

Misha sighed and sat in the leather chair. Until now, every time she thought of Ryan or his lie of a book, she felt rage and a desire to spit vitriol on his name. However, looking at this museum of the past, frozen in a moment right before they broke up, she felt great pity. People break up, and in her heart, she hoped everyone who left a relationship would grow and move onto something that was a better fit. But this room showed her that hope and reality weren't the same. Some people freeze when confronted with a challenge and never move on. The tragedy of a life like this made her tear up a bit as she allowed herself to feel empathy for the man who hurt her with his words. He'd harmed her with his lies, but in this place, she could imagine the corrosion of his heart and memories until he wanted to take something from her to staunch the emptiness. He probably wasn't trying to steal from her. It was more a weak attempt to gain something for himself. Why hadn't he moved on and created something he could call his own? There must be a nice person out there for him somewhere, who had a thing for antiques and Tarantino movies. Misha was still mad at the man who'd hurt her, but in this room full of relics, she could understand how a broken heart would seek out a target.

Her musings were interrupted when his car headlights appeared as he entered the driveway along the side of his house. Misha wiped her tears. Although the desire to run away from this house was strong, she remained seated, waiting. Waiting for the man who, according to Trevor, had something she could use.

Misha heard the front door being opened and closed. Then the hallway light was switched on. She listened to the sound of Ryan's footsteps on the floorboards. She could still recognize his steps, having a discerning ear for gaits, like a forensic scientist could identify the differences between DNA strands.

At the entrance to the living room, Ryan did a double take. He sat on the couch opposite Misha.

"Misha."

"Ryan."

"Why are you in my house?"

"I think it's time for us to discuss your book. I was hoping to get a signed copy. I figure it's the least you could do." Misha could kick herself: sarcasm was a bad fit for this person and this situation. Her emotions were getting the better of her. "Sorry, that was unnecessary. I need to talk to you, and I was afraid that if I didn't come here and wait, I wouldn't come at all. Your book nearly destroyed me, and now people are trying to kill me—literally. So I need to know why you wrote it."

"Okay. I wondered when you'd show up." Ryan looked at her like she was the ghost of Christmas past.

"Why did you write those things about me? I never wished

you ill. Ever. It broke my heart to read what you wrote. The lies were the hardest. Why would you intentionally lie about what we had?" Misha tried to keep her voice even.

"For the first three months the book was on the shelves, I expected you. I looked around every corner, and I prepared myself to have screaming fights in the grocery store or outside the gym. Then time passed. I was making money, and now I have a position of authority. I let myself forget about you and all the things in that book. Never did I expect that you'd break into my house years later." He leaned back and looked at her curiously. Misha didn't like this look or his response.

"There's a story missing in your book. I can see why you'd leave it out, but I just want to make sure you haven't forgotten it." Misha uncrossed her legs and placed both feet on the floor. "I'm going to remind you how we met. I'd been teaching at UNC for a little over a term when one day during a class, a student began challenging everything I said. He was bringing up different studies, philosophers, and points-of-view, although each was taken entirely out of context. I loved being a professor, so I treated this cocky student's arguments as valid and explained the full meaning of each of these narrowly interpreted texts. I took his interrogation without fear and taught one of my best days in the classroom, even though many students were frustrated by his inability to respect their time. At the end of class, he came up and asked me out to dinner. Do you remember what I told him?"

"You said you don't date students." Ryan's voice was softer now.

"That's right. I don't date students." Misha leaned forward. "And you told me that's fine because you weren't a student. I was so exasperated with you. You introduced yourself as one of our law professors. I asked how you were going to repay me and my students for stealing lesson time. You responded by again offering to take me to dinner. I turned you down a second time."

"I had donuts waiting for you and your students before your next class, and I brought you flowers every day for two weeks. I'd never met a woman so well-read or well-spoken. I couldn't get you out of my head." Ryan looked out the window and smiled.

"Right. But you didn't write about that or the many, many other dates we went on. Or the multiple different types of sex we had. You also left out the fact that it was all consensual and how we'd developed procedures for giving and pulling consent. I noticed these stories that would have made our relationship seem more robust and healthy failed to make it on the pages of your fictitious version of our relationship, where I played the role of villain."

They sat in silence, Misha studying Ryan's face and Ryan studying the streetlamp-lit world outside the window. Eventually, Ryan broke his reverie. "Writing about falling in love and breaking up works for heartbroken women. It doesn't sell copies of a book written by a man. At least that's what the publishing house told me."

Misha was thrown. "The publisher told you to slander me?"

"Yes and no. The book that was published isn't the one I wrote. The one I wrote has the story of how we met and all of the special moments in our relationship. My book got an agent, and it was purchased by a publishing house. They sent me an editor. She told me that if I allowed them to change the book to make it more marketable, I'd be rewarded handsomely. I trusted her, and so I agreed. I didn't know what they were going to change or how, and I didn't even ask to see proofs. You can probably guess the rest. Now, I have a great job and more money than I need. So, you were collateral damage, I guess. Why didn't you come after me? What have *you* done, Misha Campbell, that other people want you laid low?"

Misha jolted back as if punched. How could he believe that she somehow deserved the fiction he'd published? "What do you think I've done?"

"Well, I know you aren't a sincere person. You were cheating on me. When I wrote that book, it was to help myself heal. I'd thought that if I overlooked your transgressions with that blowhard Professor Martin, we could still be happy. But you left me anyway. You're a cheat and a liar, and you don't care who you hurt. But now it seems like you pulled this on someone with a lot of power, and your chickens have come home to roost." Although Ryan's tone was angry, his eyes showed the deep well of pain still inside him. He'd allowed himself to imagine the very worst of his ex-lover.

"You knew about Jeff? Why didn't you say anything?"

"Because I wanted to marry you, Misha. We were going to become a power couple. You would continue teaching until we had babies, and then you were going to host the most amazing parties and fill the room with lively chatter. We were going to be so happy together. But you ruined it, and you ruined me. Now you can live with the consequences."

Misha began to understand why there were no roommates or lovers in this man's house. "I was never going to marry you, Ryan. I'm sorry I hurt you, but I've never wanted to be a stay-at-home wife. My life and decisions were not about damaging you. I'm a flawed human who has a real struggle with monogamy. I'm just no good at it—ask my wife. But I never promised to marry you or to have your babies. We were dating, which was an agreement to feel out our compatibility over time. Everything you're saying just confirms that we weren't compatible. You have a story about us that we never discussed. You knew who I was, and you refused to accept it.

"As to getting my just deserts, your interpretation is wrong. I knew things that made publicly discrediting me expedient for some people, but destroying my credibility isn't enough for them anymore. That's why I'm here. I want your help to stop these people. I *need* your help." It wasn't the complete truth, but it was close enough for this conversation.

"Why would I help you? It could cost *my* credibility and job. And you're probably lying to me now like you did back then."

"You're still the same prick who walked into my class all those years ago. Fine. We'll do it the hard way." Misha felt her phone buzz in her pocket. There was a message from Jeff: "Immie is moving out of the safety zone and isn't answering texts." Misha shot off a reply: "Fuck. Can you handle it?" and received a thumbs-up emoji. She was thankful that Jeff had suggested using locator chips as they worked the names on the list. The text had given her a chance to refocus.

"Excuse me. I'd appreciate it if you text your boyfriend or wife or Tinder date somewhere else."

The anger in Ryan's voice told Misha that he was a second away from saying, "I'll call the cops." She needed to prevent that conversation because it would require her to break a few of his fingers, although at the moment she'd probably enjoy that. "Sorry. Okay, so let me recap. You had a dream for our relationship over fifteen years ago, and we broke up because, as you know, I wasn't happy, and I started seeing other people without telling you. Then, years after the fact, you decided to write a book to process those feelings. Most people go to therapy and figure out their part in a relationship, but whatever. Now you're sitting here telling me that I deserved your character assassination and that there shouldn't be any consequences for you. Hmm... I don't think I can unravel all this tonight because, well, people might die if I waste any more time here." Misha pulled her Beretta M9 out of the holster under her jacket and pointed it at Ryan. "I'm going to need your original manuscript now."

In his rage, Ryan thought of wrestling Misha for the weapon, but a loud voice in his head reminded him that guns are deadly. So, instead, he mumbled, "It's behind the poster."

Misha kept the gun trained on him and backed up to the doorway. This move wasn't ideal since her back wasn't covered, but she needed to be careful in case he was armed. His response was way more irrational than she'd expected, and things weren't going the way she'd imagined.

Ryan removed the *Reservoir Dogs* poster to reveal a wall safe, which he slowly opened. When Misha heard the opening click, she told him to back away, which he did, reluctantly. Now things were tricky. She didn't trust him to go into the safe, and she certainly didn't trust him behind her.

"Let's step into the kitchen for a second," said Misha. "Where do you keep your dish towels?" Misha was mad at herself for not anticipating this part of the situation or the (now obvious) possibility that her ex-boyfriend was still an angry jerk.

Eager to get into the safe and get out, Misha asked where he kept the trash bags, then used the tie handles to bind his wrists. It would be enough for now. She marched him back into the living room, moving the chair out of the way and forcing him to sit cross-legged on the floor. At least she could see him out of the corner of her eye, and it was a harder position to get out of easily.

Inside the safe was the manuscript, as well as several other items: a pistol that looked like it was from the Civil War; some financial papers; two flash drives; and a picture of Ryan's parents. Misha grabbed the documents, including the financials and the flash drives. She could send anything she didn't need back to him.

"I wish I didn't have to do it this way, but time is of the essence for me right now. I liked you a lot. But I'm sorry I didn't love you the way you wanted, and I hope you let go someday so you can find the love you deserve. Goodbye."

"Fuck you."

"Oh, before I go, who was your editor?"

"I'm not going to tell you."

Misha kicked him hard in the ribs.

"Okay, okay… it was Caroline… no, Carol—"

Misha left the way she'd arrived, circumnavigating the neighborhood cameras set up to catch dogs pooping on lawns and people stealing Amazon packages. She didn't feel good about leaving Ryan tied up on the floor, but sometimes the best place for the past was behind you, and missions can't run themselves.

CHAPTER 24

RUNNING A MISSION WAS INHERENTLY risky. Misha received a text on her way from Ryan's house. It was the message anyone running a mission hoped would never come. Whoever wanted Misha had taken Immie, and now Immie was a hostage. That left their core team down to three: Misha, Trevor, and Jeff. It wasn't ideal to have an agent taken in the middle of a massive operation against a hostile power, and less so when it was Misha's lover.

The text was simple: "Rosslyn Station, noon." The picture that accompanied it was of Immie in the trunk of a black car. Misha put away her phone and tried to focus on getting back to Jeff's house, banishing thoughts of Immie alone, hurt, and scared. A cold feeling worked down her spine and threatened to make her vomit. Even when a safe ending had seemed impossible during a mission, she'd never felt as bad as this before. This adversary had something that meant more to Misha than her own life.

It would be hard to work under these conditions, but Misha was as prepared as she could be. She and Jeff had stayed up all night working through the plan, their parts in the project, and the risks involved. So, instead of worrying about her safety or Immie's, the best course of action now was to continue focusing on the things she could control. Along with two agents, she had seventeen hours to achieve her mission.

Misha hoped that all this meant they were closer than she'd realized. They had the paper trail and the people of interest. Immie had disappeared while following the third person on the list, so she was either being followed or had stepped straight into the path of danger—probably the second, knowing her. Jeff had two of the people from the list strategically cornered. Neither of them was interested in making a move against Misha, and both were providing eyes and ears into Boardrooms K and M. Misha was relieved that Jeff was able to get them eyes and ears on the inside.

Jeff told Misha that for members of a super-secret power-hungry organization, both of the men were surprisingly quick to divulge information. He'd been suspicious, but the men had mentioned irregularities that had shown up lately. The organization was designed to prevent any one person having too much authority, yet one board member appeared to be calling the shots as of late. This information gave Misha hope. If anyone could work an asset into a helpful mood, it was Jeff. Trevor was tying up all the electronic loose ends. Misha knew they had it. If only she knew more about this board member, she had something to work with tomorrow. But Jeff needed more time to get the men to share specifics about the person they suspected. It was clear that although they were okay breaking the rules of their club, there were limits.

Without any sleep, Misha headed to Rosslyn Station by eleven. At noon precisely, the first directions came via text. This began a fast-paced rush to catch and then change trains over and over again, allowing whoever was monitoring Misha the luxury of seeing whether she had security. Meanwhile, she was getting further and further from safety. She felt herself sinking into the adrenaline brain caused by a mixture of fear and exhaustion. She had to work to keep her mind sharp by scanning the passengers to look for any possible clues.

At Metro Center Station, a woman who seemed familiar identified herself as a metro agent and led Misha into a private room. According to the agent, there'd been a tip that a woman fitting Misha's description was a possible threat. Misha received a thorough pat down and was relieved of her cell phone, wallet, and spare change. This agent then handed Misha a new cell phone and metro card and told her to take the yellow line to King Street Station.

At King Street, Misha waited about fifteen minutes before the phone rang, right as the Blue Line was pulling in: "Get off at Rosslyn." Misha jumped on, heading back to the original stop. She'd been looking for familiar faces and checking for anything that stood out, but this was a game designed by someone else. The chance of figuring it out in time was little to none. Instead, Misha hoped that her countermeasures were enough to tip things her way. It was a lot to leave on Jeff's and Trevor's shoulders.

At Rosslyn, Misha got out and looked around. On both platforms were bored, angry, or tired, people waiting for trains. Another call told her to take the Blue Line to the Stadium-Armory Station. Someone rushing behind her accidentally stepped on her ankle. This was mostly annoying, but it made following the orders on time harder.

After so many hours of crossing town, Misha thought it likely that the train hopping was coming to a close. She was right because this time, when she got off the train, a text with directions popped up on the screen. She limped about a mile past a police station and then back into a neighborhood and up the steps to a two-story rowhouse on a corner. Her ankle was throbbing now.

A woman in a business dress answered the door, and Misha

said quickly, "Thanks for having me over today, Carol. Do you have any iced tea? I feel like I've been riding that smelly subway all day, and I'm really thirsty. Has Immie arrived yet? I won't join a party before my wife. I'll wait out here until I see her." Misha sat on the stoop, with her hands in her jacket.

Misha knew she'd said too much and talked too fast. Her nerves were showing. Of course they were—she was sleep-deprived, scared, and in pain. Even so, Misha knew she'd do anything to save Immie.

The woman didn't change expression and gave only the slightest hesitation before saying, "She's in the front room."

"I'll wait here—" A flash of pain in Misha's ankle almost made her cry out. There was a lump there now, and it felt hot to the touch.

Carol knocked a pattern against the wall in the hallway, and the curtains to her left opened about half a foot, revealing Immie thrashing against her bonds.

Misha shrugged her shoulders and stood up. "Lead the way, blue jay. I'll close the door behind me."

Carol walked into the living room off the main entry, leaving the door open wide and revealing that no-one was in the doorway waiting for her. Misha closed the door as promised and stood in the doorway of the front room, looking at Carol, the station agent, and Immie. There seemed to be only the four of them in the house, but it was impossible to know for sure. Misha moved into the room with her back against the wall. She took out the cell phone she'd been given and tossed it on the couch next to Carol. "Feel free to check my work."

"I'd stop faking bravery now if I were you. We debilitated your transmitter at the station. No-one knows where you are," Carol said.

Looking at the station agent again, Misha laughed. "Hello,

Miranda. I thought you seemed familiar, but I couldn't quite place your face. You're great with make-up."

Miranda didn't respond. Just stood by the curtained window and stared back at Misha. It was Carol who spoke: "I'm very sorry it has come to this, Agent Campbell, but you are problematic, and we need to let you go."

"You aren't sorry at all, Carol. I'm bad for business. I'd hoped for a few niceties, but we're going to do this right off the bat, yes? So let's negotiate. You want money?"

"No, I want you gone."

"That's not how negotiations work, Carol. I counter your I-need-to-kill-you-to-protect-my-money with I spoke with the general last night. We crunched some numbers and brainstormed a bit. It turns out he won't be doing business with your boss anymore. Now here's where this conversation is going to get tedious, because you'll suggest that deal dies with me. And I'll remind you that I'm one of a team. I'm the only name you ever found or will ever discover. So, yes, you can kill Immie and me, but you're still out of the Boardroom, and that prominent businessman and political influencer you work for, his stock is crashing as we speak. Some very inconvenient truths about his business deals came out in *The New Yorker* this morning. Go ahead and check. Also, check your voicemail. Don't worry. I'll wait."

"I don't need to. It doesn't matter." Carol seemed unimpressed.

"Not to you, but I imagine Miranda plans on getting paid." Misha turned to Miranda, "Don't you? Of course, Carol probably intends to kill you right after she has you kill and dispose of us. It's a tricky situation. Should we all take a second to consider our options?"

Miranda took out her phone and flipped through a few screens. "I'll accept the payment transfer now, ma'am."

Carol looked at Misha and Miranda, considering her options.

She finally took her phone out of her pocket and saw many messages. It was hard to pick what to open first: her voicemail, email, or texts. She chose to flip through text messages and found enough information to support Misha's statements. "Well done, Agent Campbell. You started a few fires. But I've put out more. None of this changes what will happen to you and Immie. You had so many chances to die in the service of your country, but now you'll die a traitor's death. I'm not someone you can negotiate with."

Miranda spoke again. "The payment transfer now, please."

Carol ignored her. "It's a shame that I had to destroy you, Agent Campbell. I think under different circumstances, you would have made an excellent mentee. Max did a good job with you."

"You know Max?" Misha opted to take the bait, if only because someone talking was someone who wasn't murdering.

"Sure, I know Max. He was my instructor at Camp Swampy. That's what we called the Farm back then. We've been getting in each other's way for decades now. He's a good guy, but he's delusional in his visions for a better world. Without focused central power and control, society will fall into chaos. People need authority and fear to fall in line, but he never understood that. If he had his way, the Pledge of Allegiance would be replaced by singing Kumbaya. He was a hippie before we had hippies."

"That rings true. I can picture Max that way. So that must have been your fire at his shop?" Misha saw Carol cringe. Something wasn't quite right with the situation. Carol didn't seem bothered by the money freeze and was far more reactive to the mention of the fire.

"The fire was all Max. I tried to negotiate with him to close down the project, but he wouldn't. Measures needed to be taken."

"But your measures failed, Carol. Max didn't die in that fire."

Misha couldn't stop herself today: she was punchy in a danger-ous way.

"I'll take care of that later. Do you even get what's going on here? Miranda is going to shoot your wife, and then you. It's game over."

"I get that. What I don't understand is why. How did you find me, and why was it so important to expose me? I wasn't ever going to be an agent. I was a college professor."

Carol laughed, in a wholly unnatural way. "You were getting activated either way. Max was pushing his project forward. When Abu Ghraib was exposed, Max called the White House. Then there were the waterboarding allegations, and he started having secret meetings with senators. And then that treacherous Snowden and the others. Max was starting to present options to the joint chiefs. He was trying to get traction for his little project to go live. All of our big war 'mistakes' were Max's doing. He pulled the strings to get his operation pushed to center stage. He always makes other people feel like they made decisions, but it's always him. Not this time. He wasn't going to interfere with my hard work. So I watched his dog. I believe you call him Jeff. A FISA warrant later, and I had you. I'm sorry, but you're collateral damage."

Misha was silent. She'd prepared and angled, but it was for the wrong motivation. Carol didn't want money. She wanted power and, more, to beat Max. Finally, Misha could see the whole chessboard: it had been Max versus Carol the entire time. Just two old friends fighting it out for bragging rights, a tale as old as time.

"Of course, I never suspected you'd be nearly as good as you are. Max is an excellent instructor. I'll give him that. But you wouldn't accept disgrace, you didn't fail at the Farm, nor did you die doing your duty. So now I need to finish what he started, and then I'll have to end him. I'm sad I have to track down my old friend and kill him, but it's a means to an end."

Immie caught Misha's eye. Immie was trying to tell her something.

Misha watched her as she continued to improvise. "So you plan to kill me and then to find and kill Max? But you've already tried to capture Max once, and you failed, didn't you? You'd have a better chance of success if you used us as bait."

"You're a liability, Campbell. You dead will work just fine for me."

There was a bang. Carol fell back on a couch. Miranda spoke again. "I don't care who kills who, but I want my money, and I want to leave. Transfer it now, ma'am. Negotiations are open. Whoever pays me first gets to live."

Immie's eyes were talking now, more insistently. Misha finally got it, Carol couldn't be influenced by money, but Miranda definitely was. "Miranda, how much was she going to pay you, and can you text your account number to Jeff?"

Immie leaned back and took a breath. Misha knew she'd never hear the end of this: it was such a rookie move. Misha didn't need to motivate Carol, and it wasn't possible, but she wasn't the only person in the room with a weapon.

Miranda tossed her phone to Misha, who texted at a rapid pace. Then she gently handed the phone back to Miranda so as not to upset a woman holding a gun. Misha limped behind Immie and untied her while making eye contact with Miranda. Misha wasn't able to put pressure on her ankle at all now, but she needed to stay focused.

"I have it," Miranda confirmed. "What now, Boss?"

"We need to unarm her," Immie said, stepping in to frisk Carol and remove her weapons, while Miranda kept her gun trained on Carol. Immie stepped back, holding Carol's gun and keeping it pointed at the agent's head.

"All yours, now," Miranda said to Misha as she edged out of the room and out of the door.

Now it was just Immie, Misha, and a seriously injured Carol. As Misha was trying to wrap her mind around what might happen next, she started to see the room spin. She hobbled to the chair. For a second she thought she heard Immie asking her something from a tunnel far away. Everything turned black.

CHAPTER 25

WHEN MISHA CAME TO, IT was in a clean hospital room with a guard at the door. And Jeff was sitting next to the bed, his hand on hers. He reached up and smoothed her hair with his other hand. "Let's never do any of this again. I don't like to work this hard."

Misha laughed weakly. "What happened? What's wrong with me?" Her voice sounded strange and wooden to her ears.

"You're going to be okay. It was ricin. Carol poisoned you."

"*I'm going to be okay. It was ricin?*"

"I promise everything will be fine. Carol had done so much work against KGB and FSB that she started to adopt some of their tradecraft. You reacted faster than most people, which in this case saved your life. At first, Immie thought you were faint from seeing Carol's blood (have fun living that down), but the general told us to check for wounds, just in case."

"Where's Immie? Is she okay?" Misha had a hundred questions, but she was running out of energy.

"She's fine. Downstairs getting junk food because she says that's the only appropriate thing to eat in a hospital. But listen, when the cops hear that you've woken up, they're going to come in for your statement, which is that you were kidnapped from the Metro, you fought back, and you got away."

"How does that explain the ricin?"

"It doesn't. The doctor told them that you had 'internal injuries.'"

"Right." Misha put her hand on Jeff's arm. He was saying so much, but her head felt very heavy. As her blinks got longer, she thought she heard him whisper, "I love you."

When Misha next woke up, Immie was there. Smiling, she leaned down and kissed Misha's forehead. Misha took a long, deep breath. Everything was okay because Immie was here, smiling.

"We're safe?" Misha croaked out from dry lips.

"That's more of a sliding scale question than a binary answer. We're safe-*ish*." Immie beamed, looking down at her wife. She added, "But fainting at the sight of blood…?"

"I was poisoned."

"Yeah, right."

Two D.C. officers came into the room. Misha heard their walkies before she saw them. As she answered their questions, her exhaustion began to take over, and it wasn't long before they decided to leave her to get some more sleep. Fortunately, they weren't there long enough to dig into the very vague descriptions and contradictory details that the patient was giving them.

CHAPTER 26

BOARDROOM M WAS THE SAME as always: dingy and neglected, from another time. Max sat at the head of the table with his back to the whiteboard. Carol sat on his left, facing the door. Neither acknowledged the other's existence. Carol was silent out of pride, and Max was doing a crossword puzzle.

The door opened, and seven people filed in, at equal distance apart. They seated themselves on either side of the other end of the table. Among them was a stylish young woman carrying nine folders that she distributed to everyone at the table, except Carol. If anyone was paying attention, they might have noticed her glaring at Carol. She left the remaining folder at the empty head of the table and sat down.

A few moments later, a man in military dress entered the room, and everyone stood up. He walked to the head of the table and nodded at Max, standing opposite him. After he and Max sat down, the others followed.

The woman who distributed the folders smiled warmly at the man in military attire and said, "How are you today, Commander?"

He returned the smile affectionately. "I'm a general: it's different. But I'm well, Harper, and you?"

"Very well, Daddy. Shall we begin?"

"Yes, please." Now that Carol was apprehended, he knew Harper would be moving back into her apartment, but he wished he could think of a way to get her to stay. She'd even gotten him to enjoy that silly doctor show of hers—but seriously, Dr. Cristina Yang deserved far better. She merited a love that would last a lifetime.

Everyone opened their folders, and Harper read the header from the first sheet: "Carol's Fiasco."

The general then said, "Today begins a new protocol in how we're handling Boardroom business. Thank you to representatives from A, D, and L for your cooperation and partnership in making these changes. I know that the people in this room will continue with their tasks to make strategic updates to ensure that we follow our mission into the future. Today, we'll begin by discussing the highly unusual situation that we have before us. Please take a few moments to review the brief provided before we consider our options."

With that, everyone flipped through briefs, documents, emails, and other related notes.

A woman in a yellow sweater asked, "Do we need to read the book referenced in here?"

Max replied, "No, it doesn't provide any additional relevant information, although I hear there are still copies on Amazon, if you're interested. As for the original, we have it ready for the secure library we're creating in place of the K and L Boardrooms, now that we're combining and refreshing the meeting spaces."

The woman in yellow nodded and returned to the documents.

For ten minutes, people read and asked questions. Max and the general provided most of the answers, but each member spoke freely. Harper wrote down all the questions and answers, to be shared on the new server that was also being installed in the library. She'd found herself going back every day to check on the progress of the man developing the server. Trevor was attractive and seemed very bright, but she wasn't sure yet about his earning potential.

Finally, the general proceeded, "We have another task today. We need to determine the consequences for Carol, who's been a member of Boardroom M for decades and has served us well. However, in order to secure more power for herself, she's pushed forward an agenda that is contrary to our overall mission. While the identification of her corrupt actions has allowed us to safeguard against similar abuses in the future, we now have the unenviable task of dictating a suitable punishment. As a general, I feel her corruption meets the bar of treason, and we should eliminate the threat she poses through the most severe options open to us. Any thoughts?"

The woman in the yellow sweater said, "Agreed. She's manipulative and dangerous and acted as if she had impunity. Someone like this can't be trusted in society."

Others shared this sentiment.

Max nodded his head as each person spoke. Finally, he shared his thoughts. "I agree entirely with the mood in the room, except I don't believe we should kill people, ever. A society needs to address the causes of abuse of power and address those. We let Carol do these things, and we know what power does to people. That's why we created so many boardrooms in the first place. I think with changes, we can stop this from happening again for a very long time.

"So, I have a counter-proposal. I trained Carol and saw what she was becoming, and it would be naïve to say I was the only one who saw this. Because of this, I'd like to offer to be her jailer. She won't be in prison, but she won't have access to any form of power either. I'll take her far away from here and keep her safe. And I propose that Misha Campbell replaces me to slowly and discreetly activate my agents. She has what it takes to foster this body and our mission into the next generation."

"If not dying is the only qualification," Joshua added.

"Joshua, you've always been a stick-in-the-mud, but maybe you can be a quieter one today," the general said, with a look that drove Joshua to study his files silently. "Max, I appreciate what you're proposing for Carol, but you're older than her. What happens when you can't control the situation anymore?"

"I don't know yet, but I can figure it out."

The general looked around the room. "Okay, Max. You can have it your way. We'll give Misha your authorization, and you can leave with Carol tonight."

The ordeal was over. Max was able to stop Carol and put Misha in her rightful place. He could leave now, taking his old friend with him to where people went when they'd outlived their usefulness. Finally, his vision had moved from seeds to saplings. Misha was a worthy agent and could lead a team. The only way humanity was going to win out against weapons was to have people who could communicate and encourage each other. Max left the room with Carol, knowing that this was the hardest thing he would ever do. But it was absolutely worth it.

Trevor arrived at the hospital with Harper and two men in dark suits. Trevor carried a backpack over one arm and an attaché case in his other hand as he followed behind Harper. She moved quickly up the elevator, through the hospital corridors and into Misha Campbell's hospital room. She hated hospitals. Luckily, Misha was awake, sitting up, and joking with Jeff when they arrived. Hopefully, this meant that Misha was alert and able to work quickly so Harper could get out of the hospital.

"Agent Campbell," she said cheerily as she walked into the room with Trevor right behind her. The two men in suits waited on either side of the door. "I'm afraid I have to read you in immediately. We have a number of issues to address in preparation for the next meeting."

Misha looked at the woman and Trevor hiding sheepishly behind her. She asked Trevor, "What is this?"

Jeff answered, "Right. So there was something Immie and I were putting off telling you. Surprise: you got a new job. I'll let Harper tell you all about it." Jeff didn't mind dropping this responsibility on the new project manager. *Let Misha exhaust her anger on the newbie, instead of me.*

"A new job." Misha was confused.

"You showed such excellence in the field that you've been promoted to management. Harper can get you caught up." Jeff smiled warmly from Misha to Harper.

"I didn't ask for this." Misha looked at all of them as if this should be enough to settle the matter.

"Yes, Max volunteered you, so…." Jeff's face now froze in a smile.

"You've got to be kidding me. What has he volunteered me for?" Misha inquired.

"Well, Agent Campbell, you're now a senior board member and will need to attend meetings, starting next week." Harper responded as she took the attaché case from Trevor, unlocked it, and removed several folders. "I'll go through the materials with you today…. Trevor, the door and, you know, the stuff…" Harper gestured vaguely around the space as if that had some specific meaning. Apparently it did, as Trevor jumped into action, setting up the transmitter blocker and securing the room with a few additional pieces of tech that Misha didn't recognize.

"Max almost never went to meetings." Misha rushed to process what they were telling her.

"And you see how well that turned out," Harper responded. "Gentlemen, please." Trevor and Jeff left the room, shutting the door behind them.

"Is there any way you could just kill me?" Misha asked as Harper placed the files on her lap.

"I've been told that's exceptionally hard to do, and I'm just here until I find a rich husband," Harper countered.

"How's that working?" Misha was caught by Harper's direct approach.

"Not so well, honestly."

The women collectively sighed. Resigned to their fate of not getting what they wanted, they turned to their work.

"Max left yesterday. There have been some significant changes to procedures and the physical spaces for the boardrooms. They're outlined in the first folder." As Harper droned on about the contents of each of the folders, Misha kept telling herself this was better than being hunted.

"Pardon me," Misha interrupted, "but you seem very well prepared. Why don't you go in my stead."

"That won't work. Let me bring your attention back to this page here: all attendance is mandatory from now on. Unfortunately, I have a position on the board myself, so I couldn't fill in so you can slack off."

"I was poisoned by ricin. I'd hardly call that slacking off."

"Right. Well, they'll be discharging you by the end of the week. So thanks for your service, and it's time to get back to work.... Now this folder goes over the new plan for dividing responsibilities between the boardrooms."

It was going to take time for Misha to figure out how to get Harper to bend to her will, but she was choosing to be optimistic that she could get herself out of this boardroom business soon enough.

"Finally, this folder isn't for the meeting next week," Harper continued. "This one is personally from Max to you."

"Max left me a note?" Misha gave Harper her full attention.

"Yes, two in fact. One's a note saying goodbye, but it had a microdot on it, so I took the liberty of having it extracted and enlarged. I also took the liberty of reading both, and I believe it's a clue as to how to find the other 'designer spies'. I think that sounds nicer than 'Max's Operation'. Anyway, I'll tell you right now that you and I are the only ones who know about this last folder, and it will stay that way." Harper looked Misha in the eye. "Harper Hanover is not a snitch."

"Thanks, Harper." Misha was impressed. Harper seemed competent and reliable. Misha looked forward to getting to know her better.

"Right. Well, I don't like hospitals, so if it's okay with you, I'll leave now. One of the gentlemen can bring the locked case back to me, and Trevor will wait outside to take down the tech when you're done reading."

"Yes, that's fine. I look forward to working with you, Harper." Misha paused as she watched Harper walk to the door. Before she reached the knob, Misha added, "He's one of the good ones. He mightn't be rich, but you couldn't find a nicer guy."

Harper didn't turn around. "I think so too." Harper left and shut the door.

And like that, Misha began a new life. She'd been a professor, a wife, an object of public scorn, and a CIA agent. Now she was starting a new career as one of an elite team tasked with making the world safer. It seemed like it should feel impossible, but Misha was starting to have a good feeling about achieving impossible goals.

ACKNOWLEDGMENTS

THERE ARE SO MANY PEOPLE who do not make the sunrise every day, but they certainly make the world brighter. Ben Kirkpatrick was the first person who showed me that the world has more than enough space for all of us to shine in our own way. He has patiently unrolled plot points and character development with me every single day during our years together without complaint. I couldn't be the person I am without your unending support.

Thank you, Mom, for showing me how much people can grow and stretch to become the people they want to be. You remind me in ways big and small that Carter women can be anything because we are too stubborn to quit. Adelaide, you are the most fantastic person I have ever had the honor of knowing. You have taught me never to give up and always to brush myself off and keep going.

I'm afraid I do not have enough space to thank all those who contributed to shaping me and my work into what it is now. The amazing teachers, mentors, and people I've met along the way have given me things that each deserve a book of praise. Know that if you see this, I carry the stories of your gifts in my heart.

Four people have tirelessly picked me up and pushed me

back toward following my dream these last couple of years. First, I would like to thank Rachel Ingham and Emily McMartin, who always take my texts and are ready to help me punch up any passage that is driving me to distraction. Dave Littlechild, the person who calls me out and is never afraid to go straight to the heart of the issue. And to Meredith Hailey, who fills my soul with delight and love. I couldn't make it through most days without you, and I am forever rich because of your friendship and support.

Finally, two people will never be able to read this, but I would be remiss if I didn't acknowledge them: Betty June Kiley and Jerry McMartin. You both gave me gifts that allowed me the resources and the inner strength to be the person who could work hard to reach my dream. I love and miss you both.

ABOUT GRETCHEN KIRKPATRICK

Gretchen Kirkpatrick is a daydreamer with a rich background of imaginary professions from a dinosaur veterinarian to spy. Currently, she is busy imagining being with her friends and family while she waits out COVID-19 from the safety of her home in San Jose, California. Boardroom M is Gretchen's first published novel. Currently, she is editing the sequel and trying to convince herself that she wants to blog for her website instead of encouraging plants in her garden to grow faster.

Connect with Gretchen
www.gretchenkirkpatrick.com